TOBY AND THE

SILVER BLOOD WITCHES

by

Sally Doherty

Published by Soaring Skies Publishing

Formatting by Let's Get Booked

www.letsgetbooked.com

Cover illustration and map design by Sarah Jane Docker

www.sarahjanedocker.com

Print ISBN: 978-1-9196259-0-4

eBook ISBN: 978-1-9196259-1-1

Ten percent of the profits from each book will be

donated to the ME Association.

For my mum,

for everything

SMI
CAR PARK
TOBY'S HOUSE
MRS WINTERBERRY'S HOUSE
NO MANS LAND

A BAT'S EYE VIEW OF TOBY'S STREET

SMI GATES

TREE CLOSE

CHAPTER ONE

One more sleep. One more day at school. Then the whole of the summer holidays to keep an eye on Mum.

Toby lifted the glass to her lips, and she sipped weakly.

"Thanks, love."

"Are you going to be too hot under the duvet?" He wiped his brow. This heatwave had been going on for days.

"I'll be fine."

Toby perched on the edge of the bed. If he made sure everything was quiet and peaceful, if nothing unexpected happened, Mum would be able to rest. Then maybe she'd get better. There was a chance, right?

The floorboards creaked in the attic above, and his mum flinched. "It keeps doing that today."

"The windows are open, remember?" said Toby. "It's probably that."

He turned to close the curtains. Light spilled from the room onto their patio below with its rickety bench and plant pots full of weeds. At the bottom of the garden, the hedge loomed out of the darkness. It was high and thick to keep people out from what lay beyond. On the other side, a lamp flickered in the building.

Toby drew in a sharp breath.

A girl stood at the distant window, her long golden hair illuminated in the light from the lamp. *That was strange.* Surely all the workers would have gone home by now? Despite the hot July evening, a chill crept through Toby's bones. *This could not be happening. Not again.*

He forced himself to look away. Above, the night sky was clear. Behind him, his mum's breathing was shallow and laboured, her frail body almost swallowed by the plump pillows.

It was no use, he couldn't resist. His gaze strayed to the window as if the girl were a magnet. She was staring right at him.

A memory scratched at the back of Toby's mind and images swam into his vision. *A woman ... a woman at the window* ... No! He had pushed her out of his thoughts for so long. He would not remember her now.

"Toby?" his mum whispered from the bed.

He yanked the curtains closed.

"Is everything OK?"

"Fine!" Toby flicked off the light and hurried out of the room before his mum could ask more.

CHAPTER TWO

Fifty-four minutes to go. Only fifty-four minutes. Toby fidgeted at his desk the next day, willing the maths teacher to arrive. Shrieks and laughter swirled around him. He checked his watch again. Fifty-three minutes to go. Just this last lesson and then six whole weeks off. No more school. No more Bull's Eye Bean.

Dacker sauntered past, giving Toby a sharp nudge. "Holidays aren't going to be much fun for you, are they, Bean?" he sneered. "Got to look after Mummy, haven't you? I bet they take you away one of these days. A kid shouldn't be doing all that stuff."

It was the longest speech Toby had ever heard from Darren Dackman, and an icy hand gripped his insides. But he had no time to respond. From behind came the sound of paper being crumpled: Dacker and his gang were beginning their favourite game. Instinctively, Toby reached for the tuft of white hair which grew at the nape of his neck.

Beside him, his best mate, Roger, squirmed in his seat. "You could always dye it brown like the rest of your hair. Get them off your back," he whispered.

Toby raised his eyebrows. "Yeah right."

The paper missile, crushed into a tight ball, bounced off his shoulder. The gang jeered at whoever had missed.

"Hold still, Bean!" shouted a rough voice. Then a pencil sharpener hit him hard on the back of his head. With that force, it could only be Dacker's right-hand man, Boz, twice the size of the rest of them, who had thrown it. Sure enough, Toby heard his whoop of delight, "Bull's Eye!"

Toby didn't turn round. He never did. But he knew the great oaf would be celebrating, arms in the air, as if he'd won an Olympic gold medal.

Roger shifted and glanced behind.

"Ignore them!" Toby hissed.

"Doesn't it bother you?" asked Roger.

Toby shrugged. "There are worse things to deal with."

"You don't care about anything anymore! Not since your mum ... well you know."

Toby glared at his friend. What did a stupid pencil sharpener matter when his mum ... He stopped himself. *Don't think. Don't feel.* That was his survival tactic.

Usually it was best not to retaliate when the gang was on the rampage; it only made things worse. But today was different. In an hour, Toby would be free from Dacker. Today was a chance to do something. As Boz continued to clown around, Toby scooped up the pencil sharpener from the floor. He passed it from one hand to the other, deciding. Everyone held their breath as the sound of Mr McClean's footsteps tapped up the corridor. Toby hurled the sharpener at the blackboard several metres away. It ricocheted off and flew into the wastepaper bin with a satisfying clunk. The girls' giggles turned to appreciative murmurs and Roger's cousin, Jazz, cheered. The teacher entered the room before Boz could respond. *One to Toby.*

The maths lesson finished and the bell rang; school was over for another year. Chattering excitedly, the class gathered up their belongings and streamed into the sunshine.

"Are you sure you can't come tonight, Tobe?" Roger asked, spinning a football in his hands. "It is the holidays."

"I've got to get home. Get Mum a drink. She hasn't seen anyone all day. You know that!" said Toby.

"You'll be there tomorrow though?"

"Of course!" He'd never miss the Saturday kickaround – the only time he could forget about everything, thinking only of the ball and where to pass it next.

"Good! I want Player of the Year on *my* team this week," said Roger.

"That was over two years ago!"

"I'm sure you'd still be Radton's best striker if

you could get there."

"Well, I can't."

Roger threw the football at Toby who deftly returned it.

"Oof!" exclaimed Roger as it thumped him in the chest. "Nice!"

"You need to work on your reaction skills!" Toby dodged out of the way as his mate tried to clout him on the head.

"See you tomorrow then," yelled Roger and he raced after the rest of their mates to the park.

Toby trudged home, the heat from the sun baking the pavement under his feet. Reaching the entrance to Fir Tree Close, he stopped at the solid metal gates. They were as high as a house and as thick as a wall. Beyond lay the SMI, the building behind Toby's garden. People said the initials stood for Solar Material Investigation, but that was all Toby knew. He'd lived on this road his whole life, twelve years now, yet he still couldn't pass without staring, without wondering what mysteries the barrier concealed.

Toby had managed not to think about the girl at the window all day, but now his thoughts went to what he had seen last night. Why had she been in the SMI? Maybe he'd imagined her. That was what he'd told himself the previous time. The time he'd done nothing. Light and dark could play tricks on your eyes, couldn't they?

Could he have imagined somebody at the window twice though? Could he have imagined a woman staring at him, a woman screaming … *Don't think about it. Don't think about it.*

Footsteps echoed behind Toby, and he turned to see Jazz bounding up. He'd known her as long as he'd known Roger, and that was pretty much forever. The three musketeers, or so they had been once. Jazz might be Roger's cousin, but sometimes she felt like Toby's too.

She gave his shoulder a playful push. "Nice throw earlier! It's about time that lot stopped pushing people around."

"It's not like the five-time champion of dodgeball would miss a shot," said Toby, puffing up his chest and giving a wink.

"Whatever." Jazz poked him in the ribs.

They looked up as a powerful BMW roared past and pulled into the entrance to the SMI. For a moment, Toby was blinded, dazzled by the reflection of the sun on the gleaming paintwork. A tinted window slid open, and there was Dacker, sitting in the passenger seat. He raised his arm and flung a crumpled ball of paper, hitting Toby on the chest. Slowly, the gates whirred open and the car purred through.

Toby and Jazz peered into the grounds, making the most of this rare opportunity, but there was little to see. The grass was carved into lawns with razor-sharp edges and not a blade out of place. Beyond stood a

13

two-storey concrete building, a dark and silent silhouette against the sky. Then the gates clanged shut, enclosing the private world once more.

"How come Dacker's allowed in the SMI?" asked Jazz, her brown eyes wide.

"No idea. I think his dad has a high up job there. I was never allowed in when Mum was a cleaner."

"I wonder if Dacker knows what they do?"

"I doubt it. The employees aren't allowed to talk about their work. I was never able to get any details out of Mum."

"I can imagine you tried! We never used to be able to get you to shut up, you were a right chatterbox." Jazz paused and fiddled with a stray wisp of her black hair. "How is your mum, by the way?"

Toby grunted and scraped the toe of his shoe along the pavement. Silence fell.

"Anyway, I think you're right," said Jazz after a moment. "Dacker can't know anything. He'd be so full of himself if he did, he wouldn't be able to keep it to himself. Can you imagine? He'd tell Boz and then the whole school would know."

The paper Dacker had thrown lay in the gutter; Toby gave it an idle kick. It began to unfold revealing Dacker's untidy lettering scrawled across the page. Toby picked it up.

Meet me at the park midnight tonight.
I have something you will want to see.

14

Do NOT bring anybody with you.
Be there or else.
You have been warned.

Toby's heart sank. What on earth could it mean? This was definitely not part of his summer plan.

"What does it say?" Jazz leaned in to get a closer look.

"Nothing," answered Toby.

Before he could pull the note away, she grabbed it and scanned the writing. "Don't go."

"Mmm," he grunted. "Might be worse if I don't."

"Then I'll come with you."

"Better not, it says not to take anyone," said Toby. "I'll be fine by myself."

A loud rumble echoed around the neighbourhood. Dark clouds were looming on the horizon.

Jazz slung her schoolbag over her shoulder. "Got any plans for the holidays? See you around?"

"Maybe."

"Maybe. Maybe. You hardly ever go out anymore! We're having a big family party next week. You should come."

Toby hesitated. A party with Jazz and Roger would be fun. Their Mauritian families were always so welcoming. So different to his own quiet house. But it didn't feel right to go. "I can't leave Mum."

Jazz shot him a sad smile and dashed off in the other direction, her ponytail flapping up and down.

Another boom of thunder sounded overhead. Toby hurried past the towering SMI gates and several red brick houses until he reached number twelve.

CHAPTER THREE

Toby leant forwards till he was almost breathing on the screen. His striker raced up the pitch, the ball glued to his foot. Toby stabbed at the controls and he swerved in and out of the defenders. GOALLL!

"Toby, are the attic windows still open?" his mum called weakly from the next bedroom as heavy raindrops beat the roof.

He plummeted back to earth. Since arriving home from school, he'd fetched his mum a cup of tea, scrubbed the beans off last night's saucepan and stuffed his dirty clothes into the washing machine. This had been his first chance to sit down and he was on the verge of winning the World Cup. But it couldn't be helped. This was simply the way it was.

"Toby?" Mum called again. He wrenched himself out of his chair and hauled himself up the ladder on the landing to the room under the eaves. Here, the three musketeers had built Lego fortresses, fought dragons and rescued princesses. Nowadays, their games were packed into a pile of dusty boxes. It had been years since Toby had used his train set. His time was taken up with more pressing issues and there was no longer any place for fantasy worlds.

Giant cobwebs stretched across the corners of the attic. Toby shuddered. What size spiders could have woven *them*? He turned to see a box on its side and his train scattered across the floor. That was odd. Surely it had been tidied up long ago? *Get a grip.* He was not going to start imagining spiders large enough to knock over his toys.

Puddles were forming on the attic floor. It had been a muggy few days. A record for July, the headlines declared. The windows had been open for a while and had at least created a breeze through the house to keep Mum cool. He'd better close them though, before those puddles became ponds and he had something else to sort.

As Toby prepared to launch himself down the attic ladder, a slight movement in between the boxes caught his attention and he hesitated, straining to see in the stormy evening light. Nothing there. He turned to leave when he remembered the strange noises of the previous night. There had been creaking above his bedroom ceiling. Just box lids rustling in the breeze, right? But what if it was something else? His eyes flicked again to the overturned train. Did they have mice? Or rats?

A bolt of lightning suddenly illuminated the attic, and Toby's stomach almost fell out of his bottom. There, behind a box overflowing with Lego pieces and in front of an old toy garage, lay a bundle of brightly coloured rags. Out of the top of the bundle peeked a face with squinting eyes and a button nose. Then the attic went dark again.

Toby dived for the light switch and watched in horror as the head swivelled to look at him. It was not a pile of rags at all. It was the body of a large woman covered in a multicoloured patchwork dress. A woman lying on a black cloak. And, more to the point, a woman lying in his attic. A finger rose and pointed at him. Toby yelped and leapt backwards, only just preventing himself from falling down the ladder hole.

"Keep away from me!" hissed the head.

Toby swallowed hard. "Who are you?"

She glared at him.

"What are you doing in my attic?" He tried again.

"*Your* attic? This is where I stay now." Her voice was husky and she coughed loudly.

There came a faint call from below. "Toby, is everything OK?"

"Err … yes, fine, just looking at my old things," Toby stuttered and turned back to address the problem in front of him. He took a deep breath, trying to steady the tremble in his voice. "I don't know who you are or what you want, but you have to leave."

The woman pointed an accusing finger again. "You Earthens shot at me. This was the first place I saw, so I dived in."

Earthens? Shot at her?

"And now I'm stuck here." She lifted the hem of her long patchwork dress to reveal her swollen ankle, tinged with blue. Toby winced.

How the heck had she got up the ladder with a twisted ankle? And without him or Mum noticing?

A small bell jingled below. Toby glanced at his watch and cursed. 7pm. He should already have started cooking dinner. His stomach clenched; he couldn't leave now, not with this stranger in their attic. And he certainly couldn't tell Mum, she had enough to worry about.

He looked up to see the woman ripping a yellow patch from her skirt, leaving a gaping hole. Grimacing, she wrapped the material around her ankle, then smoothed out her dress.

Toby blinked. Where had the hole gone? There had definitely been a hole, hadn't there? Or maybe not. There was no gap now in the red, yellow, purple and blue patches, all jostling for position. His head swam with confusion and his heartbeat quickened.

The bell jingled again. "Coming!" he called through gritted teeth.

"Do not tell anybody about me!" The woman tried to edge forwards but uttered a cry of pain and clutched her ankle.

Toby backed away further. "Why?"

"My life is in danger!"

Shooting one last look at her skirt, Toby put a foot on the top rung of the ladder. At least she couldn't move with that ankle.

"I need food!" she called as he disappeared from view. "And I don't suppose you have any pondweed wa …?" Her final words were lost in the tumult of rain drumming against the slanted windows.

CHAPTER FOUR

Toby gazed into space, taking no notice of the plate balancing precariously on his knees, the blackened edges to the fish fingers, the dried out shells of peas. He'd cooked dinner in a daze, his mind preoccupied by the strange woman in their attic. Forgetting the potatoes, he'd hastily added some bread and hoped Mum wouldn't comment. They always ate in her bedroom; Mum propped up with pillows and Toby perched on a chair. This was usually the only time of day she had energy to talk, but they were saying little this evening.

Through the window, a large satellite dish rotated slowly on the top of the SMI roof. The device searched the sky, a telescope sticking out from its centre. It was on the lookout for signs of new planets, so Toby's neighbours said. Beyond the thick hedge at the end of his garden, there existed a metre of 'No-man's-land', enclosed on the other side by a ten foot, barbed wire fence.

Why was the place so secretive? The memory from two years ago scrabbled at Toby's thoughts again. *A woman screaming, hammering at the window, crying out for help.* Fear pulsed through him as it had done on that night. *Ignore it.* Toby dragged his attention away from the window, forcing the images from his mind. He drummed his fingers on the arm of the chair and pushed the fish fingers round his plate.

"Is everything OK, sweetheart?" his mum asked in her quiet voice.

"Fine!"

"You seem a little distracted."

Toby grunted.

"You would tell me? If something was worrying you?" she continued. "I hate that you have to do so much around the house. I wish you didn't with all my heart."

His mum reached out to touch his hand, but Toby withdrew it sharply.

"Everything's fine!" he repeated.

Everything, however, was far from fine.

It was 11pm before Toby could venture up to the attic again. After saying goodnight to his mum, he waited an hour in the hope she would have fallen asleep and not hear his footsteps on the creaking ladder. He negotiated the steps as silently as possible, yet still they rattled. In one hand Toby balanced a plate, in the other a glass, and between his teeth he carried a torch. He'd become adept at climbing to his attic playroom when he was younger, his arms full of snacks and fizzy drinks.

Perched at the top of the ladder, Toby peered into the gloom. He hated the dark; who knew what could be lurking in the shadows? But he couldn't pull the light switch in case it woke Mum. Maybe the woman had just been a creation of his imagination, and there would be nothing in the attic, save the familiar faded boxes. Unfortunately, that wasn't the case. Toby's feeble torch picked out the woman lying exactly where he'd left her four hours ago. His stomach lurched.

The woman blinked several times and covered her face in the unexpected beam of light. "Sizzling serpents!" she exclaimed.

"Shh!" Toby put one finger to his lips and gestured downstairs. "My mum's asleep ... or was."

He moved the torch so its light fell to one side of the woman, illuminating her in ghostly gleam. Toby's chest tightened. Hauling himself off the top of the ladder, he edged forward into the attic and pushed the plate and glass towards her.

"I should think so!" she said. "Leaving me alone without food and drink for hours!"

"You shouldn't even be in my h ..." Toby trailed off. Was that a twinkle in her eye?

The woman gulped down the glass of water, then surveyed the plate with suspicion.

"It's just fish fingers."

"Fingers of what?" The woman wrinkled her nose.

"No, no. Fish covered in breadcrumbs."

"Fish?"

Toby frowned. "You know … they swim in the sea."

"Oh!" said the woman as if that made everything clear. "We don't have them at home." She pointed upwards. "No sea in the sky." With a yelp, she clapped her hand over her mouth. "I'm not supposed to tell you that!"

The more she talked, the more Toby felt as if he was falling headlong into a curious fictional world. He needed to take charge of the situation, before it completely spiralled out of control.

He took a deep breath. "You can't stay here. Let's get you down the ladder and I'll help you return to your house … or wherever it is you came from."

"I don't think I'll fit through that hole."

"Well how did you get here in the first place?"

"Why, through the window." She indicated to one side of her.

The torch beam picked out something which had previously escaped Toby's attention: a broomstick on the floor. Its middle had splintered in half, and only a single sliver of wood held the two parts together.

Suddenly, there was a movement on one of the roof rafters. Something small and black hurtled through the air. It swooped at Toby's head, claws raised, fangs blazing, veered around and swooped again. Toby threw his arms up to shield his face and dived to the ground. He dropped the torch, and everything went black.

"Barnaby!" shrieked the woman. "Barnaby! Are you listening to me? Stop that right now!"

When Toby could no longer feel the rush of wings, he flicked his torch back on. *Phew, it still worked.* "What was that?" he spluttered, lowering his arms.

"That's Barnaby," said the woman proudly. "He's my fluttermouse."

"He's your *what*?" Toby stood up, his heart still hammering from the unexpected attack. *Please don't let Mum have woken up.*

Toby stared at the creature hanging upside down from the woman's shoulder. Was that a *bat*?!

"Don't worry." The woman lowered her voice. "He's a sweet little thing really." She reached out to stroke the winged creature on its chest but rapidly withdrew as the bat bared its teeth. Barnaby gave a disgruntled squeak and plunged headfirst into a pocket on the woman's black cloak. He wriggled around and then, still upside down, buried himself in a corner.

"So, where were we? Oh, yes, my broomstick." She regarded it sadly. "I crash-landed, you see. I was in such a hurry to get away from the … well … anyway … so it's not currently in working order."

Toby closed his eyes and tried to gather his thoughts. He was still reeling from the sudden, vicious greeting from the bat. Furthermore, it was getting late, and his mind was becoming as jumbled as the patches on the woman's dress.

"So, you were travelling on a broomstick?" he said eventually.

For several long seconds, she eyed him, scrutinising him intently as if she could see into his soul. Then she spoke. "Toby, I hope I can trust you."

This unexpected use of his name unnerved him. *How did she know that?* A shiver ran up his spine.

"You may be an Earthen, but I need your help. My niece is in trouble." Her voice wavered.

The woman was in Toby's attic, knew his name, wanted his help, yet he still didn't have the slightest clue who she was or where she had come from.

"My wand, it slipped out of my sleeve just before I flew through your attic window," she continued.

She was bonkers. Totally and utterly barmy.

Toby stood up straight, attempting to seem braver than he felt. "Well, why don't you go and look for it then?"

"Ah, I'm stuck here till I can mend my broom and for that I need my wand. So you'll have to find it for me."

Toby dug his toe into a crack on the wooden floor.

"It's very urgent," she pressed.

"I won't find anything tonight, it's pitch black," he said. As if to prove his point, the torch flickered a few times and went out, throwing them back into darkness. Toby shook it and flicked the switch a few

27

times – nothing happened. He edged away; he didn't trust the woman, especially when he couldn't see her.

"Well as soon as it's light, can you search for my wand? I think it fell in your garden." Her disembodied voice floated through the gloom.

Toby pondered this for a few moments. Maybe he should help her – if it meant she would leave. His eyes were becoming accustomed to the dark and he could make out her faint outline. "I'll look for it when I wake up," he said firmly.

After a few seconds, the woman nodded. "Very well. And remember, don't tell anybody about me!"

"But why? Why is your life in danger?"

She drew in her breath, clearly considering the best way to answer. "We have to keep our existence secret," she explained. "Some see us as a threat, a threat that needs to be controlled, even eliminated. You yourself already know too much. Do not betray me."

Toby picked his way through the shadows towards the top of the attic ladder. The woman obviously lived in a fantasy world inside her head, a world that was becoming more fanciful by the minute. He made a decision – he would have a half-hearted attempt to look for this so-called wand just to placate her. Then, when this came to nothing, he would contact the local police station, and they would take the matter, that is the woman, off his hands. Toby gave a small smile; soon everything would be back to normal.

CHAPTER FIVE

As Toby pulled off his trousers, something rustled in his pocket. He pulled out a ball of scrunched up paper. Dacker's note! He'd forgotten all about it. Sitting on the side of his bed, he reread it.

Meet me at the park midnight tonight.
I have something you will want to see.
Do NOT bring anybody with you.
Be there or else.
You have been warned.

He didn't want to go, of course he didn't. But the last two lines reverberated in his head. If he didn't go, would the repercussions be even worse? It was already quarter to midnight – he needed to get a move on.

Wearily, Toby pulled his trousers back on and tiptoed down the stairs. The air was cooler than in the daytime, but he barely needed his jumper. The whole road was asleep; all the houses and their residents tucked up for the night. He'd never been out this late before. The world was silent and eerie: no cars, no planes, no people. His footsteps on the pavement made the only sound.

As he passed the SMI gates, he was struck with the memory of his mum punching her entry code into the panel. She'd smiled and waved as he headed to school. That was the last day she'd made it to work, over two years ago now. The image still tormented him every time he passed.

At the corner of Fir Tree Close, a figure stepped out. A real figure this time, not one living in his memory. Toby shot three feet up in the air.

"Sorry!" whispered Jazz.

"Jeez!" cried Toby. "What are you doing here?"

"I thought I'd come along. Keep an eye out."

"I told you. I'll be fine."

"Are you sure? I could come just in case."

"No!" Toby pushed her away.

She stalked off, and a twinge of regret shot through him. He hadn't meant to be rude. But he could handle things on his own, he was used to it. And Dacker's note had warned him to go alone.

Reaching the park, Toby found a metal padlock hanging around the gates. He gave them a rattle – they were firmly locked. He peered into the gloom beyond; there was no way he was going to venture into the dark. Who knew what traps Dacker could have set up? A whistle pierced the night air, and Toby turned to his right to see two figures sitting on the swings in the light of a lamp post. They gestured for him to join them. He glanced around. There was nobody in sight, nobody to catch him trespassing. Taking a breath, Toby flung himself at the gate. He got a good foothold and clambered upwards. Soon he was scrambling down the other side. Keeping his eyes on the ground, he approached the two figures, stopping by the entrance to the kids' playground.

"Don't be shy, Bean! Come and join us!" cried Boz as if they were old chums.

Dacker smirked. He was a boy of few words (other than the occasional snide remark), yet he exuded a menacing air. A sly snake about to strike. And when he did, it was his sidekick and second-in-command, Boz, who usually performed the dirty work. There was not a soul in the school who ever wanted to be the target of *that* lumbering gorilla.

Toby shuffled forwards, the woodchips scrunching under his feet. Stopping by the see-saw, he regarded the two of them, his heart pounding. Dacker slid off the swing and strolled towards him. Boz sauntered behind. They were both taller than Toby, and Boz's thickset frame oozed danger. What the heck did they want? There was no one around. If they decided to beat Toby up, nobody would stop them. He swallowed hard and held his ground.

Dacker held out a black object. Toby tried to take it, but Dacker kept a firm grip. "It's a video camera – from the SMI. Watch the screen."

On the camera, Toby saw two people, two very

familiar people. His mouth fell open as he watched his mum wobble out of bed, her hair knotted and unkempt. She leant on Toby as he helped her stumble across the room.

What? Dacker had filmed them? How? It must be from an SMI window. That was the only place where you could see inside his mum's bedroom. But how had he seen so much?

"It has a good zoom function, doesn't it?" sniggered Boz.

How dare Dacker? HOW DARE HE? Toby trembled with rage. He made a grab for the camera. Dacker was too quick and whipped it out of reach.

All of the anger that had built up since his mum fell ill, all of the emotion he'd suppressed, flared up inside Toby. He lunged at Dacker, fists flying. With one swipe, Boz sent Toby staggering backwards. Hands clenched by his side, Toby stood red-faced and panting, glaring at the two of them.

"Calm down," said Dacker softly. "There's something we need you to do. As long as you follow what we say, then there's no need to worry."

"But if you don't, we'll show the video to the whole of the school!" crowed Boz with a stupid grin.

"And then the authorities will take you away, when they find out how ill your mum is, what you have to do for her," sneered Dacker.

A cold fear flooded Toby, like ice rippling through his bloodstream. He wouldn't be taken away

… would he? "What do I have to do?" he muttered through gritted teeth.

"You'll see. Meet us here, midnight tomorrow."

Toby edged backwards, keeping his eyes on the two boys.

"Oh, and in case you were thinking about trying to get the video camera," added Dacker, "I'm taking it back to the SMI tomorrow for safekeeping."

Toby burst into a run, tackling the park gate as effortlessly as the hurdles in P.E. Fuelled by fury, his feet sped onwards; street after street flashed by unnoticed. Reaching home, he pulled up short. Still his temper raged. He couldn't go in, he wouldn't be able to keep quiet. Tearing a rock from the garden, Toby hurled it at the fence. It made contact with a satisfying crash. Then the fence post broke in half. *Great.* Another thing to sort out. It was a good job Mum slept at the back.

Toby sat on the doorstep, trying to calm down. The thought of people watching the video wrapped a cold hand around his insides. He couldn't let anyone see it, see his mum so weak and vulnerable. She would be distraught; she'd lost enough dignity already. Dacker's words raced round his head on repeat, '*And then the authorities will take you away*'. Toby could *not* let that happen. His home! His mum. He belonged there, and she needed him. He needed to deal with this the way he dealt with everything else: don't think, don't feel, just do.

He would have to meet Dacker and Boz at midnight the following night.

CHAPTER SIX

The next morning, Toby awoke with a start. He hadn't dropped off for hours the previous night, his thoughts spinning with the day's events. Couldn't he be free from Dacker even in his own house? And then there was the stranger in the attic. In Toby's sleep, a large chuckling woman had chased him, brandishing a broomstick. Ferocious bats swooped through the air, and sticky tendrils of cobwebs tried to entrap him.

Now, feeling unrefreshed and, with a head still full of strange dreams, Toby caught sight of his clock. Nine o'clock! School! He tried to leap out of bed, only to find the duvet coiled round his arms and legs. He wrestled to free himself from its clutches, but the more he thrashed, the more tangled he became. It was as if it had a mind of its own. "Stupid thing!" Toby gave the duvet an angry thump. Why was he so irritated these days? He knew he was becoming increasingly grumpy with Mum, yet he couldn't seem to stop. Toby took a deep breath and let it out slowly.

It was only when he swung his legs to the floor that his befuddled brain remembered that a) it was

Saturday and b) it was the holidays. With a relieved sigh, he sank back onto the pillows, but he couldn't relax. He rubbed his eyes and glanced at the clock again, better fetch Mum her breakfast.

Toby dragged himself out of bed and stumbled across the room, tripping over the clothes he'd discarded the night before. His schoolbooks were stacked in teetering piles that threatened to trip him up further. Football trophies lined his desk, their once shiny surfaces covered in a thick layer of dust. He couldn't bear to look at them these days. He tried to keep the rest of the house tidy. It was important to Mum even though she never saw it. However, his bedroom was his space. Who cared if the carpet couldn't be seen beneath the jumbled clothes, books and football posters?

Fifteen minutes later, Toby and his mum sat eating breakfast quietly in her bedroom, her brown hair spread across the pillow and her skin pale in the light from the window. Toby shared her colouring, her blue eyes as well as her hair, but she was already more petite than him, and he still had some growing left to do.

A photo frame sat on his mum's bedside table. A grinning Toby stared out at him. His tenth birthday. Mum had thrown an amazing football party that year. She'd spent hours decorating his cake. When the icing turned everyone's tongues bright green, they'd laughed so much it hurt. The photo annoyed him nowadays. *Remember what a fantastic time you used to have? Remember how happy you both used to be?* it jeered. It was just five days after his birthday that everything had changed.

Toby leafed through his football magazine but couldn't concentrate. He glanced at the photo again and then at the empty space next to it. "Why don't we have any photos of Dad?"

"You know why." Her voice was tired; she barely had the energy to talk in the mornings.

"I can't even remember what he looked like."

"We've been through this a hundred times – I'm sorry love, I don't want to be reminded."

Toby knew this. He knew it upset her, yet he couldn't seem to help himself. "We have nothing in the house that was his. Nothing! And when I think of him, all I see is a shadowy figure."

His mum sighed. "He had your hair. He was stouter than you though and more broad-shouldered. You get your body shape from me."

"Did he have a white tuft of hair too?"

She paused. "Yes, he did. I know you don't like yours, but he was proud of his. He thought it made him unique. Just you see, people will think you're intriguing when you're older."

Toby scowled. Right now, being different was just asking for trouble.

They lapsed into silence. Toby wanted to ask

more, but he'd pushed it enough. He went back to munching his toast. The dry crumbs stuck in his throat and he forced himself to swallow. Through the window, the SMI beckoned to him. *A girl with shimmering hair. A woman screaming.* He buried his head in his magazine, though he didn't take in a word.

"Thanks sweetheart," his mum said as he cleared away her bowl.

"Another cup of tea?"

"No, I'm fine. What are you doing today?"

"Not sure." Toby hastily left her room.

He carried the remains of breakfast down to the kitchen, unlocked the back door and stepped out into the bright sunshine. *Now to the small matter of a crazy woman in the attic and her imaginary wand.* It was going to be another warm day, but yesterday's rain had cleared the air, and it felt fresher.

Toby didn't start his search immediately, in case inquisitive neighbours were watching and wondered what he was up to. He began kicking his football around. He rarely did this anymore – on Saturdays at the park, he and his mates got straight into a game. Toby was rusty, but he could still keep the ball off the ground for ages. The actions felt so familiar, and an unexpected warmth filled him, as if he'd been wrapped in a comforting blanket. No doubt Mum would hear him playing outside; she had ears like a bat. Lying in bed without other distraction, she seemed able to home in on whatever he was up to. It was unnerving. She'd be pleased to think he was having fun though.

However, kicking round a ball was not what he was here for. He had a wand to find (or not). Giving the football a hefty boot, it flew thirty foot through the air till it hit the high hedge at the bottom of the garden. Toby sauntered casually after it, his eyes roaming from side to side, scouring the grass for any sign of a ... well, what was a wand supposed to look like? Some sort of a stick? It was lucky he'd mown the lawn a few days ago – he wouldn't have found anything in their normal jungle. Mum had been pestering him for weeks to cut the grass; it wasn't until it was knee-high that he'd succumbed. Kicking the ball again, Toby continued to scan the ground, but there was no wand to be seen. *No surprise there then.*

He wanted to take something to the woman as proof he'd tried his best. He hunted for a stick, but there weren't any trees or bushes in their garden. It was best that way – the fewer plants, the less work. There were some pots dotted around the patio and in the side beds. However, without Mum's care, their flowers had long since died. Toby glanced around the neighbouring gardens. A small tree grew next door. *Just the thing.* Now, was Mrs Winterberry at home? If she spotted him, that nosy busybody would certainly wonder why he was picking up a stick in her garden. Toby went back into his house, through the kitchen and into the lounge to check out the front.

On the way, he threw a cushion onto the sofa that

he'd knocked off the previous evening. He touched the red fabric with a sad smile. He and Mum had spent weeks decorating this room before she fell ill. It was a shame she never saw it now. The cream for the walls and carpets, with red for the furnishings had been her idea; she'd wanted it to be modern yet cheerful. It was weird, he'd forgotten what a happy person she used to be.

Toby peered out of the front window – Mrs Winterberry was on her drive. Her short dark hair bobbed as she walked, although 'walk' wasn't how he would describe it. She always looked like she was hurrying, even trotting, as if she were late for a bus or being chased. As usual, her eyes darted around the neighbourhood. Little escaped her attention.

Perfect. She was just going out.

Toby hurried back through his house and into the garden where he began knocking his football around again. On the third kick, he sent the ball soaring upwards, aiming for Mrs Winterberry's garden. As the ball descended, Toby held his breath, desperately hoping it wouldn't fall into SMI territory. Down it fell. Down, down, hitting the top of the high hedge … and bouncing into his neighbour's garden.

Phew, he thought, letting out his breath.

And "Whoops! Silly me!" he exclaimed out loud, giving his forehead a theatrical smack for the benefit of any onlookers.

Toby scurried to the end of his garden where he

squeezed between the hedge and the fence. Well, that was his intention. However, either he or the hedge (and probably both) had grown since he'd last had to retrieve a ball from next door. And so, after pushing for a few seconds, he found himself wedged between hedge and fence. Branches spiked into his face, and a splinter speared his leg. Why on earth had he agreed to go on this wild goose chase? Why was he going to so much trouble just to take a stick to a barmy woman in his attic? But it was now no easier to go back than forth, so he might as well continue.

Beating back the hedge with his arms, Toby tumbled into Mrs Winterberry's garden. Unfortunately, it was the hedge that came off the better from their encounter, leaving Toby with scratches on his skin and without a piece of his T-shirt sleeve. He looked up to see a patch of white material hanging amongst the branches.

Drat. Mum wouldn't be pleased if she found out. They had enough money to live on, but they had to be careful. When she'd first fallen ill, Mum had been full of worry about their financial situation. She'd said they might even lose their house. Then the letter had arrived. Toby wasn't sure what it had said, something to do with insurance payments. Most importantly, they could stay at 12 Fir Tree Close.

Standing in Mrs Winterberry's garden, Toby was acutely aware he was trespassing and more conscious than ever of the white patch of hair at the back of his head. It seemed like a beacon, brightly signalling to any onlookers that here Toby was. His hand strayed to the nape of his neck, trying to flatten down the tuft, but it never was one for behaving.

Toby poked around the bottom of the tree at the end of the garden. There were no sticks to be seen. Why hadn't he thought about this before? Summer wasn't exactly the time of year for twigs to blow off trees. His football had hit the hedge and bounced several metres up the garden. Wandering towards it, Toby's spirits sagged – he would have to return to the woman empty-handed.

Then something caught his eye, something glinting in the grass. He leaned over to get a better view. It was thin and cylindrical, about twenty centimetres long. At first glance, it appeared to be made of metal, gleaming in the morning sun. However, when he picked it up, the stick took on a different appearance. With Toby's back to the sunshine and the object in shade, it was cream rather than silver, more like ivory than metal. This couldn't actually be what he was supposed to be looking for, could it? His mind wasn't prone to flights of fancy; these days he kept his imagination firmly under control. *Don't be ridiculous Toby. Wands and magic do not exist.* So he reined in his thoughts before they could fully unfurl their wings and take flight.

Still, at least now he had something to take to the woman as proof of his efforts to help. Picking up his football, he straightened up. He was pushing the stick into his left sleeve, when there came a shout. "Toby!"

He jumped, dropping his ball and only just stopping the stick from flying out of his sleeve. Mrs Winterberry was watching him from her kitchen door, her hands on her hips and a sour expression on her face. Toby had been so absorbed in his discovery, he hadn't realised she was back. How much had she seen?

The heat from the sun suddenly felt much stronger, and the colour in his cheeks rose. Being friends with Roger, however, Toby had become an expert at talking his way out of scrapes.

"Sorry, Mrs Winterberry!" Toby called. "I was getting my football."

"You'd best come round the front." Her tone was sharp.

With her hair going grey, she was probably in her late fifties, but Toby didn't know much else about her. While she seemed very interested in other people's business, she kept her own life private. She'd moved to the street a couple of years ago, yet Toby had never learnt if she had family or what her job had been. He'd never dared to enquire either; she had such a prickly air about her, like a porcupine thrusting out its spines.

Toby picked up his football and followed Mrs Winterberry down the drive by the side of her house. His hand clutched the stick in his top, willing it not to fall out.

By her front garden, they paused. Toby glanced

up, ready to say goodbye, and his heart skipped a beat – she was staring at his sleeve. Mrs Winterberry's eyes swept upwards to meet his own. It happened so quickly, maybe she hadn't been looking at his sleeve at all. Just because Toby knew he was concealing something strange did not mean it was lit up with lights and visible to the rest of the neighbourhood. Mrs Winterberry seemed about to say something, but before she could speak, Toby gabbled out a quick apology and fled. He ran down her drive, along the pavement bordering their two front gardens and up his own drive, all the time under his neighbour's watchful gaze.

In the privacy of his kitchen, Toby removed the stick from his sleeve and examined it. It looked and felt like nothing he'd ever come across before. It was neither smooth nor rough, heavy nor light, cold nor hot. He lifted his head and stared into space for a few moments. Then, he held the stick aloft and pointed it at a glass. "Move!" Nothing happened. Toby gave a half laugh, half grunt of ridicule and threw the object onto the kitchen work surface.

The wall clock emitted a loud tick: the large hand had hit the twelve. It was ten o'clock – he'd better take the woman some breakfast. Cereal was not a good idea, he'd be sure to spill the milk while climbing the ladder. Toast too was out of the question; Mum would smell it and wonder why Toby was eating again so soon. Little could happen in the house without

Detective Mum being aware. The woman would have to make do with bread and strawberry jam. As he spread the jam, Toby contemplated how he should best go about telling the police there was a crazy woman in his attic.

CHAPTER SEVEN

As Toby clambered up the attic ladder a few minutes later, Mum called his name. No doubt she'd want to know why he was going into the attic again, but he'd run out of excuses. So he put his head down and pretended he hadn't heard. He'd have to tell her soon enough anyway, if he was to get help to remove the woman.

Sun streamed through the skylights, and, in full daylight, the woman looked younger than Toby had previously thought. She was tapping her thigh in an agitated manner – hardly surprising since she was stuck in the attic, able only to await his return. As he appeared at the top of the ladder, her head, its chestnut hair pulled into a bun, snapped upwards. Toby flinched in her sudden stare, then stepped into the attic. He scanned the rafters for signs of the bat, he didn't want another surprise attack. The creature was nowhere to be seen; probably still curled up in the woman's pocket. Her eyes lit up at the sight of breakfast, but on glimpsing what Toby held in his other hand, all thoughts of food were forgotten.

"My wand! You found it!" she cried in delight, reaching out.

"It's just a stick ... or a piece of wire." Tentatively, Toby held it out. As the stick came into contact with the woman's fingers, it trembled, and a small electric shock surged through Toby's arm. He let go and jumped backwards. *What the ...?*

The woman smiled gleefully. "It missed me!" she crowed. "There, there." She patted the stick as if it were a living being.

Toby frowned. Had the stick really quivered when it touched the woman? Or had he imagined it? Was it that he was feeling shaky anyway that morning?

"Now, first things first!" Still sitting, her injured ankle spread out in front, she faced the broken broom lying by her side and raised the stick. Her stomach gurgled loudly. She hesitated, before turning back to Toby.

"Well, maybe I should have a bite to eat first." She took a mouthful of bread and munched hungrily. "Mmm ... moonberry flower?"

"Jam! Strawberry jam." How could she not know what jam was? And what the heck was moonberry?

While the woman chewed, she pondered Toby's answer as if it were a new concept to her. "Tasty," she concluded as she swallowed. Still holding the half-eaten slice of bread aloft, she raised the stick over the broom and began chanting:

Mend this broom
Entwine the wood
Straighten the bark
And make it good.

Toby raised his eyebrows. What a ridiculous rhyme. Yet, every cell in his body quivered. The sensible voice inside his head reminded him there was no such thing as magic, but he couldn't help wonder, would something happen?

On the final word, the woman gave a small flourish of the stick and pointed it at the broom. The splinters flattened and the two halves of wood grew into one. The woman beamed. Then, with a loud ping, a piece of bark flew from the broom and landed at Toby's feet.

Her smile fell. "I never was the best at magic." She examined a splinter which once again protruded from the handle.

It probably hadn't helped matters when, midway through the chant, the woman had rescued a stray morsel of jam from falling off the bread. With a strawberry in her mouth, the second half of the spell had become somewhat incoherent. If it *was* a spell, that is. Toby wasn't sure what he had seen. He thought the broom had been in two halves, but perhaps it had been a trick of the light. Had the broom really joined? Toby didn't want to believe his eyes. Magic didn't exist, and yet, if it did, then his whole grasp of the world turned on its head.

The woman could see he wasn't convinced. "Why don't you wish for something?" she said brightly.

"Wish for something?"

"Yes. What do you want? I can magic it for you."

What did he want? WHAT did he want? Wasn't that obvious? He didn't even need to think for a second to know the answer to that question. It was at the back of every thought, hanging heavy on every breath he took, every movement he made.

"I want my mum better." Toby's voice was cold and monotone. This was dangerous territory. The land of wishes was a place where you could gain hope, but where hope could be stripped away, leaving you torn to shreds. It was a land into which he did not stray.

"Oh Toby." The woman looked crestfallen. "I'm so sorry." Her gaze returned to meet his. "That's one of the things our magic can't do. With ill health, we have to let nature take its course."

Toby turned away. *Stupid woman! Some kind of magic that is.* He never let people see how distressing Mum's illness was for him. Why had he said anything! It was as if the cocoon he'd worked so hard to build, the cocoon which shielded him from despair, had been peeled away. Tears formed in the corners of his eyes, and he blinked them back furiously.

The woman attempted to change the subject. "How about a drink of pondweed water?"

Toby ignored her. A lump stuck in his throat and

he didn't dare speak.

Placing her empty glass on the floor, the woman directed her stick at it.

Fill this glass
Right to the top
With pondweed water
Drop by drop.

Toby couldn't help but watch. Slowly but surely, the glass filled from bottom to top with a murky, green liquid. In fact, it became so full, it overran, and the thick fluid oozed in rivulets down the outside.

"Flapping fluttermice!" muttered the woman as small, stagnant pools formed on the floor.

Toby barely noticed. He was still staring at the glass as if in a trance, his eyes unblinking and his mouth open. Time had slowed down, and every second was long and surreal. Suddenly dizzy, he sat down with a bump, grateful for firm ground beneath him. The room rocked like a small boat on a choppy sea, and Toby placed both palms flat on the floor to steady himself.

The woman watched him silently. As he slowly recovered, his dazed brain began to work again, and time regained its normal speed. *What had he seen?* The woman had not touched the glass. The end of the stick had been a foot away from it, and yet the glass had filled with liquid. Toby's heart beat faster, and now time seemed to speed up; his thoughts racing through his head.

Magic exists! It really exists. Excitement burst through his normal self-control. He jumped to his feet, unable to keep still. "Magic exists!"

The woman grinned. "Here, have a sip." She held out the glass.

Toby froze. As if in a theatre when the curtain falls, the atmosphere changed abruptly. In that split second, he realised her power and he shrank backwards, unsure of her once more.

Oblivious to his change of mood, the woman shrugged. "Well, no point in letting it go to waste." She gulped it down. Sighing with contentment, she wiped her mouth with her hand, leaving a green frothy smear on her lips. "Mmm … my favourite. Not as good as the real thing, of course. Magical food and drink never are. But not bad, not bad at all."

"Would it work for me?" asked Toby, keeping a good distance from the woman.

"Work for you?"

"Your stick." He still couldn't bring himself to call it a wand. "Would it work for me?"

"Oh no. Certainly not."

"Why not?"

The woman held the stick up and regarded it as if it were a precious gem. And it did look like a jewel as it glittered in the stream of sunlight. "Well, a wand only works for its owner, the person who made it. And only witches can make them." Her eyes widened as if she were about to tell him a great secret. "Many things go into a wand, you see. A feather from a whiskered snow owl, a petal from a moonberry flower, the bark of a willow tree, not to mention a strand of hair and a drop of silver blood from the witch herself. These must all be joined in a small pond under a full moon."

Toby snorted. *What a load of rubbish.* That said, he'd thought the same thing about magic itself until a few minutes ago. But he couldn't prevent himself being drawn back to the safety of reality, already he was beginning to doubt what he had seen.

"Now," said the woman. "We've wasted far too much time."

'*We?!*' thought Toby.

"My niece is in danger and I must summon help."

Toby nodded his head. Once and for all, he would seize control of the situation and get rid of this woman. "Well, you have your wand and your broom is mended so you can go back to wherever you came from."

"Oh no. I don't think that's a good idea."

"No?" Toby squeaked. *Stupid voice!* Why had it chosen now to betray him? It was as if it sensed his fear.

"No," said the woman. "It'll be much quicker if I call them. Besides, they'll need to come here themselves."

"They? ... Here? ..." Toby echoed.

"Yes, I'm sure our Head Witch at least will want

52

to come down."

This was getting out of hand. Toby drew a deep breath and pulled himself together. He would *not* let her direct the scene. He had to act now before he became completely entangled in this web she was spinning.

"I'm afraid you must leave." He folded his arms. "My mum needs quiet. Stress worsens her condition, and she will be on edge, wondering what is going on."

"I'm sorry, that's not possible, Toby. We may need your help, and besides, this house provides the ideal location."

"But ..."

"Now, you won't be able to hear my conversation."

"What?!" This was preposterous. She was in his house, he had brought her food and drink and had even found her wand for her. And now she was cutting him out?

"Sorry, I've already explained – the more Earthens know about us, the more dangerous our situation is. I'm going to create a soundproof wall, so if you could move back a few paces." She motioned with her wand for him to retreat.

With clenched teeth, Toby edged away. It was the gesture with the wand that had done it. He should probably obey her. How powerful was she? Visions of being turned into a frog floated into his mind. But he dispelled them. *This is not a fairy tale, Toby.*

CHAPTER EIGHT

"Now, where's my warbler?" The woman pulled on a chain that hung around her neck, revealing a disc at the end of it. It was round and flat, no bigger than a drinks coaster. Clutching it in one hand, she directed her wand at the space between her and Toby and began chanting:

Build me a wall
Through which no sound
Can resonate
Above nor round.

A ringing sound buzzed in Toby's ears as if the pressure around him had changed. In front of him, there was a hazy quality to the air. With an impatient sigh, he knelt down.

The woman held the tip of her wand to the disc and squinted into it. After a minute or two, her body relaxed and she began to speak. At least, it looked like she was speaking, but no noise filtered through. She did indeed seem to have created a soundproof wall.

Even though Toby couldn't hear her, he stared at the gabbling, gesticulating woman. Who knew what she could be saying? He still didn't trust her. He needed to pay as much attention as possible. Toby tried lip-reading but was unable to make out a single word. Who was she speaking to? How many other witches were there, if that was what she really was? Images of hordes of witches formed in his mind. *Don't think. Don't think.*

An age passed, and still the woman talked. It was strange to be this close to the scene yet unable to hear it. Toby's concentration waned. It was like trying to remain interested in a television programme without the sound. He drummed his fingers on the floor until he realised it might be disturbing his mum. His attention drifted. It wandered away from the woman into the corners of the room. Those were big webs – where were the spiders that had spun them? That was one good thing about having a resident bat; maybe it would eat them. Toby's stomach rumbled, and his mind wandered further, down to the kitchen to the contents of the fridge. He was contemplating whether he'd prefer a ham or cheese and pickle sandwich for lunch (although it was far too early) when his attention snapped back into the present moment. Something had changed. What was it? He could hear the woman! So her earlier confession had been correct – she wasn't particularly skilful at magic.

Still talking animatedly into the disc, she didn't

seem to have noticed. As she spoke, her eyes flicked to Toby. "He's a bit grumpy, but I've heard him with his poorly mother. He cares well for her. I think we can trust him; he found my wand for me. What other chance do we have? He's our only hope."

She was talking about him! *The cheek!* Toby's ears burned and he glowered at her.

With the words, "I await your arrival," the woman finished her conversation and withdrew the tip of her wand from the warbler. She flourished her wand to remove the now non-existent soundproof wall and smiled at Toby. "There!" she said brightly, oblivious to his flushed face and glare.

"So?" asked Toby.

"So?"

"So, what's happening?" he said with exasperation.

"Ah yes. Well, Witch Willow, our Head Witch, and one other will be arriving in an hour or so."

"And why are they coming? You mentioned something about a witch, your niece, in danger?"

"All in good time."

She was so frustrating! "If you want to use my house, if you want my help, you'll have to tell me."

She nodded yet said nothing.

Toby's mobile beeped in his pocket. It wasn't an expensive phone, they couldn't afford that, and he had to limit his usage, but Mum was adamant he should stay connected to his friends. It was a message from

Roger: 'Where r u? C u in the park?'

What time was it? 10.45am. *Drat!* He was supposed to have met Roger at the roundabout five minutes ago. This must be the first time Toby had ever forgotten a game of football. Usually it was the highlight of his week. Should he go? He was in the middle of such a strange situation. Who knew what might happen next? But his friends needed him for equal teams, and he didn't want to let them down.

"I have to go out for an hour," Toby said. "Can we move you downstairs, out of my mum's earshot?"

The woman regarded her swollen ankle with uncertainty. "Well, I suppose I could fly down … if you can help me stand up?" She held out her arms.

Toby recoiled. She waved them in the air and gave him an encouraging nod. He shuffled forwards. Her palms were sweaty in the heat, and his toes curled. He pulled and tugged, and their hands squelched and slipped together. At last, she stood balancing on her good leg, swaying from side to side.

Toby dried his hands on his trousers with a grimace before picking up the broomstick and passing it to her. She sat astride it, avoiding the splinter, and let out a sigh of relief as she took the weight off her injured ankle. Toby scrutinised the space above and below the broomstick. Was it really hovering in mid-air?

"Oh! My cloak." The woman pointed at the black bundle where she'd been sitting. "Mustn't forget that;

I'd stand out like a red Retrieagle in this dress if my bubble burst."

Toby handed her the cloak. There were so many things about her last sentence he didn't understand, he didn't know where to start. Before he could collect his thoughts, she'd wrapped the cloak around herself and was flying towards the open skylight. She hung on tightly as the broom twisted and turned to pass through the window. Toby had visions of the woman bouncing down the roof and plunging headfirst onto the patio. But then she was through the opening and had quite simply disappeared.

Toby ran to the window and peered out. The skylight was high. However, if he stood on tiptoe he could just get his chin over the rim. Outside there was only the bright blue sky: the woman had vanished. Toby gripped the bottom of the window frame. He felt like he was teetering on a thin line between reality and … and what? Reality and madness? Reality and magic?

He shook his brain to clear it, but the image of the woman flying through the window and vanishing danced in front of his eyelids. There was no denying it this time. Magic really did exist.

"Toby?" came his mum's faint call as he clattered down the ladder.

Toby bit his lip. She would want to know why he kept climbing up to the attic. What on earth could he say? He popped his head around her door with what he hoped was a casual air.

"What's going on?" she asked wearily.

"Nothing."

His mum frowned. "I may be ill, but that doesn't mean I'm stupid. Don't think I didn't hear you banging around up there in the middle of the night last night. And who have you been talking to? Are you on the phone to Roger?"

"Um, yep. But nothing's going on, Mum. We were just arranging football."

"Look, I'm glad if you have plans to see your friends. It'll do you good to get out a bit. But I haven't forgotten the things the pair of you used to get up to before I fell ill."

Toby widened his eyes innocently.

"Don't pretend you don't know what I'm talking about. That boy lives with his head in the clouds. Always dreaming up another great escapade. What about that giant slide?"

Toby suppressed a smile. Roger had found a lengthy piece of plastic in a skip and persuaded Toby to help him cart it home. The slide started at his bedroom window, balanced on the edge of the conservatory roof and ended in a paddling pool full of water. On Roger's very first attempt, he slid down at terrific speed, whooping as he went, flew off the end and missed the paddling pool. He landed in the garden rockery, breaking his arm, not to mention his mum's favourite flowerpot.

"I want you to have fun, sweetheart. I really do. My illness shouldn't stop your life too," Toby's mum continued. "Just no broken bones, OK? No broken anythings for that matter."

"Don't worry! Everything's fine."

"Hmm…"

Scurrying down the stairs, guilt flooded through Toby. He hated lying to Mum. But the guilt annoyed him. It was hardly *his* choice to be caught up in this crazy situation. It was definitely like being trapped in a giant spider's web. The more he struggled to extricate himself from its sticky mesh, the more entangled he became. And the more time he spent with the witch, the larger the web grew.

Toby hurried down the hall to the kitchen and opened the door. The woman wasn't there.

"Well move aside then! Let me in!" exclaimed a voice right in front of him.

He jumped backwards.

As she passed through the door, the woman sprang into view.

"H … how did you do that?" said Toby.

Still holding her injured ankle aloft, she toppled onto a chair. "How did I do what?"

"I couldn't see you!"

"Why, I was in an invisible bubble of course."

An invisible bubble?

Toby's phone beeped again. "I have to go. I'll be back as soon as possible. Why don't you watch TV while I'm gone?" He switched on a small television set in the corner of the kitchen and handed the woman the remote control.

She gaped in wonder as a picture of two people flicked onto the screen. "Two tiny people! In a box!"

"No, it's just a picture." Toby rolled his eyes. *How primitive were the witches?*

She looked confused. "But how does it work?"

"Well ..." *How did it work exactly?* Toby wasn't sure. "A programme is broadcast to all houses in the country. Anybody can watch this by turning on their television."

"But how?"

He ignored her. "I have to go now. Please keep quiet – I don't want my mum to know you're here. She can't get down the stairs, so it shouldn't be a problem."

"What is the matter with your mother, Toby?" asked the woman kindly.

Toby hated this question. His stomach clenched into a tight ball. He did not go to this place. He could not go to this place. He looked after his mum, he did what he had to, but he never ever thought about it. To think was to sink; to fall into a bottomless pit of despair.

"She's just very ill," he said through gritted teeth and headed for the door, leaving the woman engrossed in the television.

CHAPTER NINE

Toby hurried home. Football had been disappointing. For the first time ever, it had not provided the release from reality it usually did. He'd played poorly, distracted by the morning's peculiar proceedings. Only a few minutes into the game and he'd begun to regret having left a strange woman unsupervised in the house.

Let's face it, Toby. She's a witch. You've seen it with your own eyes. You've left a witch alone in your house with your mum ill in bed.

If only he could tell Roger, give some release to the strange ideas spinning in his head. But the woman had begged him not to, and for the moment he would do as she'd asked. At half-time, Toby made his excuses and fled, leaving Roger watching after him with a puzzled expression.

As he neared home, Jazz cycled up behind. "So, how did last night go?"

"Last night?" Toby was startled. *How did she know about the witch?*

"With Dacker and Boz!" exclaimed Jazz. "What

did they want?"

Of course. He couldn't believe he'd forgotten about the video. But the events of that morning had eclipsed everything else.

"Um, nothing."

"Oh, obviously. They wanted you to meet them at midnight in the deserted park for nothing," said Jazz with exasperation. "Just be careful, alright? I can help if you tell me what's going on."

"They want me to meet them again tonight," Toby blurted out. He bit his tongue. *Why had he said that?* He didn't want anyone else to know about the video of Mum.

"Want me to come?"

"Nope."

Jazz let out a frustrated humph and sped off, pedalling fast.

Toby need not have worried about the witch. He burst through the back door to find her exactly where he had left her, still hypnotised by the television. She hardly noticed as he poured a drink, before throwing himself onto a kitchen chair to gulp it down.

The doorbell rang sharply, jerking the witch from her trance. "That'll be them!" she cried.

"Why did they ring the bell? They'll alert my mum!" Toby opened the front door to find nobody there. He frowned before remembering to step aside. Although he was expecting it, he still flinched when two women materialised out of thin air, right next to him. Toby put his finger to his lips and ushered them down the hall.

"Just someone trying to sell something," he shouted up the stairs, closing the kitchen door behind them.

The two women made a striking pair. The first had a mass of orange curls which sprang from her head like a magnificent mane. She was so tall and her hair had such volume that it brushed the top of the door frame as she entered. Next to her, her companion appeared tiny.

"You did right to call us, Bumble," said the first.

The witch from Toby's attic smiled broadly.

So that was her name. It certainly suited her.

"Toby," said Bumble, "this is Witch Willow and Witch Hazel." The first gave a slight nod while the other offered a small but friendly wave.

It was obvious which of them was the Head Witch. It wasn't just Willow's height which gave her presence – she exuded a quiet air of authority. Her face was unreadable, neither stern nor overtly friendly. It bore no wrinkles, no lines. It was as if she never betrayed great emotion. She was impassive with a touch of the formidable.

As Toby examined the Head Witch, she herself scrutinised him. He shifted uncomfortably under her penetrating gaze and turned his attention to her companion. While Witch Willow looked older than

Bumble, Witch Hazel was much older than them both. She was so small, she made Toby feel oversized. She smiled warmly at him, her papery skin creased with wrinkles, and her eyes twinkling behind spectacles perched on rosy apple cheeks. A bun held her white hair in place while stray wisps floated around her face.

Witch Willow cleared her throat. "Toby, we need to ask you some questions."

He was taken aback. Why did they want to ask *him* questions? He was the one in need of answers! "Um, OK, but can everyone please talk quietly – we mustn't disturb my mum."

"I'll soundproof the room." Willow circled the kitchen with her wand, reciting the same words Bumble had chanted earlier.

Should he explain the soundproofing spell had not been particularly successful that morning? No, he got the impression the Head Witch's magic would not fail.

The kitchen, not large in the first place, felt cramped with its four occupants. The two newcomers removed their black cloaks and laid down their broomsticks, before seating themselves at the wooden table in the centre of the kitchen. Beneath their cloaks they wore dresses as did Bumble. But there the comparison ended, for their dresses were neither as flamboyant nor as shapeless. Witch Hazel wore a lilac dress with buttons up the front. Willow's dress matched the colour of her grey eyes. It fell to her feet and, at the neck, rose in a high collar, framing her face.

Still wearing his football clothes, Toby straightened his dishevelled top and rubbed a muddy patch on his shorts. An ominous sensation trickled through his bones. It was like he was about to be interviewed, or worse, interrogated. He was outnumbered, and they had a power he could not match. Three witches, three wands, one Toby. Why hadn't he stuck to his original plan and informed the police? He'd become sidetracked by magic and, he had to admit it, curiosity – was he about to finally find out why Bumble had been in his attic?

Toby," said Willow, "tell me about the building at the back."

"The SMI?"

"The one with the large gun on its roof."

"That's not a gun," said Toby. "That's a telescope."

"It's a gun!" cried Bumble. She was silenced by a withering look from the Head Witch.

"SMI? What does that stand for?" asked Willow.

"Solar Material Investigation," answered Toby. "Nobody knows what it does. Not even the workers can talk about it."

The witches gave each other knowing glances, and Toby felt left out of a big secret.

"Bumble, perhaps it's time you told Toby your story," said Willow to the witch at her side before turning to Toby. "You understand it's very dangerous for Earthens to know about the wyline clan? We have

66

to keep our existence secret for our own safety. We are disclosing this information to you only because we have to, because we may need your help."

Toby grunted a non-committal reply. They made it sound like they were doing him a favour! At what point would they understand he didn't want to help, couldn't help?

"Bumble?" prompted Witch Willow.

Witch Bumble swelled with pride at the prospect of being the centre of attention and the one to reveal her story to Toby. "I was in my house in Little Witchery when …"

"Please excuse me a moment, Bumble," interrupted Witch Willow, "but perhaps I should first briefly explain our history to Toby." She turned to address him. "For many centuries," she began, "witches lived on land amongst Earthens. Throughout this time, we were a persecuted race. You have heard perhaps that suspected witches were often drowned or burnt at the stake? Gradually, our wyline ancestors fled society and established small colonies in remote areas. Their lives remained, however, in danger, and so it was that they built a town in the sky; a new home where they hoped they could be safe and free."

"In the sky?" Toby raised an eyebrow.

"Sky hooks!" exclaimed Bumble triumphantly as if this would explain everything.

"Bumble, you may continue your story," Willow instructed.

"Now, where was I?" muttered Bumble. "Ah, yes, there I was, having a bit of a sit down when I saw Skylark, that's my niece, hurrying past my house. She was up to something. I was sure of it. Fifteen years old and a bit of a tearaway, when all's said and done. 'Going through a difficult phase,' her mum says. Skylark was clearly on her way somewhere, and what's more she'd got her broomstick with her. So I followed, grabbing my own broom on the way out. She was heading straight for the outskirts, with me always a bit behind. To be honest, it was hard to keep up. And then, after we'd walked down a few roads, quite suddenly she vanished. Talk about shocked!"

"Making yourself invisible is against wyline code," said Witch Willow.

"But it's the only way to see another invisible person," continued Bumble, "being in a bubble yourself. So I had no choice but to turn myself invisible too. As Skylark approached the exit to Little Witchery, I finally worked out what she was up to. Before I could stop her, she'd tiptoed past the witch on guard and disappeared through the hole." Bumble shot an apologetic glance in the direction of Witch Willow, not daring to meet her eyes. "I'm sorry, I can see now I should have told the sentry. At the time, all I could think about was not getting Skylark into trouble. And so, instead of calling for help, I too flew out into the evening sky." Bumble trailed off. "I'm not much good in a crisis."

Patting Bumble's arm, Witch Hazel cleared her throat and spoke for the first time since her arrival. "Travelling alone outside is forbidden," she explained in her soft, gentle voice. "In the past, witches were allowed to leave the town on occasional forays, providing they were in small groups. Even this is now rare. It's not safe. You did well, Bumble, to notice Skylark was leaving." Hazel paused in thought. "Many years ago, my grandmother lived on land. Her small wyline community lived in constant fear of Earthens. The tales she told!" Witch Hazel looked lost for a moment, far away amongst her memories, then her eyes returned to Toby. "Young witches today complain of being trapped and having no freedom. They don't realise how lucky they are to have the sanctuary of Little Witchery." She gave a sigh and a small smile.

Bumble picked up her tale again, seeming more confident after Hazel's kind words. "The dusk was drawing in. To the east, I could see nothing but shadows. I scanned the sky for Skylark. And there she was, a small black figure on the western horizon, silhouetted against the final rays of sun. I sped towards her, but she was travelling so swiftly I couldn't catch her. She didn't notice me. In fact, she was oblivious to everything. She adores flying, does Skylark. She soared and swooped through the air on her broomstick like a bird. Yet all the birds were safe in their roosts, as she should have been too. It was as she lost height, that I realised the true reason for her outing …"

A small bell tinkled above. Toby cursed. Sometimes Mum had the worst timing. Despite his annoyance at the witches' invasion of his house, he found himself riveted by Bumble's story. He ignored the bell and let Bumble continue.

"A few years ago, Skylark's younger sister, Witch Daisy, went missing." Bumble suppressed a sob.

The bell rang a second time. Toby couldn't ignore it again. He heaved himself to his feet and headed for the stairs. There was a whoosh as he broke the soundproof wall and air was sucked back into the kitchen.

"Make sure you have a good lunch after all that racing around in the park, love," said Mum, when he appeared at the bedroom door. "Can I have mine at half past one please?"

"OK. Do you want me to eat up here?" asked Toby. She liked him to eat with her, when he could; his company gave her a small break from her solitary existence.

His mum studied his preoccupied face. "No, don't worry about me, I'm fine."

Toby jogged downstairs. The witches had thirty minutes to carry on with their explanation before he had to take Mum her lunch. The murmur of voices filtered along the hall – Willow had forgotten to re-soundproof the room. It sounded like they were disagreeing about something, but Toby couldn't quite make out the words.

"… have to put … first." Was that Witch Willow's voice?

And then Hazel. "Not very fair on …"

The conversation didn't make any sense, and it stopped as soon as he entered the kitchen. Willow was standing by the sink, scrutinising the view beyond. She regarded Toby thoughtfully then reseated herself between her two companions.

Delighted to have her audience back, Bumble plunged straight into her tale once more. "Flying so close to Earthen territory, I knew Skylark was looking for Daisy. We've searched countless times, but we've never found her. She would be eight now … still so young. Skylark loved her little sister more than anything." Bumble shot a glance at Willow before whispering, "I admire my niece for being the only one who hasn't given up."

Witch Hazel put a comforting hand on her shoulder. "Tell Toby what happened next," she said gently.

"Skylark was flying far too low: she couldn't have been more than ten metres from the ground." Bumble's voice quivered. "I was racing towards her when a small ball flew out of *that* gun." The witch pointed a plump, accusing finger in the direction of Toby's hedge behind which lay the SMI. "It struck Skylark on her back, and she fell to the earth. She lay there on the grass, as still and as lifeless as a rag doll." Bumble's face crumpled. "I tried to rescue her, I really did!" she choked. "But another ball flew out of the gun and missed my ear by a whisker. I swerved, flew over the hedge and dived through the first window I saw. And that's how I ended up in your attic."

As it built towards its crescendo, Bumble's tale had held Toby spellbound. Now it was finished, he fell back to reality with a bump. It couldn't really have happened, could it? His earlier misgivings about the witches returned. And then he remembered the girl, the girl he'd seen at the SMI window two nights ago. Was that Skylark? Were the witches telling the truth after all?

"But why would the SMI want to shoot down a witch?" Toby frowned.

"We've been worried for some time that Earthens have become aware of our existence," replied Willow. "Perhaps they shoot because they fear us. People are often scared of outsiders, of those who are different. They react without trying to understand more. We intend no harm. We do not believe in violence. We wish only to be able to live freely."

"So, you want to try and rescue Skylark?"

"Well, you see …" Witch Willow shifted in her seat and looked uncomfortable.

"What?" Toby's eyes narrowed.

"We think that this telescope, this gun, may be a witch detector. That is to say it can detect the presence of witches. If this is the case then we need somebody else, an Earthen to …" Willow hesitated.

Toby sensed what was coming next. So this was why the witches were taking so much trouble to explain everything. They wanted him to rescue Skylark! "No way, absolutely not," he replied.

Jeez, it was hot in the kitchen suddenly. Toby fanned his face with the top of his T-shirt.

"But my niece is in grave danger!" burst out Bumble.

"Anyone would be a fool to break into the SMI," said Toby. "They'd get into so much trouble and besides, it's impossible to find a way in."

Witch Willow glanced to her left. Toby followed her gaze till it rested on the three broomsticks leaning against the kitchen side.

"No way," he repeated. "Absolutely not."

CHAPTER TEN

Half an hour later, they were all assembled in the back garden. Willow waved her wand over Toby and chanted:

> *Grow him a bubble*
> *Let him not be seen*
> *Keep him from trouble*
> *With invisible screen.*

As soon as Toby was invisible, he could see the witches in their bubbles too. Witch Hazel and Witch Bumble stood by his side, Bumble leaning heavily on her broomstick to take the weight off her injured ankle. It was a peculiar sensation, being invisible. Everything around Toby had taken on a misty hue. It made him feel distant from his surroundings, like the time he'd tried on Roger's glasses.

Suddenly, Bumble let out an almighty sneeze.

"Shh!" Toby glanced at his mum's bedroom window.

Barnaby shot out of Bumble's pocket and landed

in Mrs Winterberry's tree. Toby eyed him with caution.

Bumble rubbed her face. "'Scuse me, I have a touch of the Summer Snizzles."

"Summer Snizzles?" said Toby.

"Yes, pollen gets right up my nose."

"Oh, you mean hay fever."

"No." Bumble shook her head firmly. "Summer Snizzles."

In front of them, Willow mounted her broomstick, ready for Operation Witch Detector. "You never know," she said to Toby, "if it doesn't detect my presence, you might not need to help after all."

He gave her a stony look and said nothing.

Witch Willow rose into the air and glided down the garden. From where they were gathered, Toby couldn't see the SMI. Willow cleared the hedge with a metre to spare and then swerved to the left. A black ball, the size of a tennis ball, came flying over the hedge. Toby ducked as it whizzed over him and hit the wall of his house with a clunk. Just in time, he turned back round to see Willow careering up the garden towards them. He dived to one side as she skidded to a halt. Since her arrival, Witch Willow had been a woman of composure and dignity, so it was strange for her to be so flustered and unkempt. Her cloak hung from one arm, her voluminous hair sprang more wildly from her head, and the front part of her broom had broken off.

"Well," she said, once she had regained her breath, "I think we can safely say that it's a witch detector." The three witches regarded Toby as if waiting for him to speak. He stared at the ground, scuffing the soil with his trainers.

"It might not just detect witches," he said eventually. "It probably detects the presence of anyone."

"That is exactly what you can help us to find out," replied Witch Willow.

Drat! Toby had been meaning to show he probably couldn't approach the SMI either. Instead, he had managed to enmesh himself further in this spidery web the witches were spinning.

Fifteen minutes later, Toby, Willow and Bumble left the house and headed for the park. Hazel had insisted on staying in the safety of Toby's house, protected from the Earthen world. The two witches followed Toby in their invisible bubbles, Bumble shuffling along with her swollen ankle, using her broom as a walking stick.

"Don't stop suddenly," whispered Willow. "If we bump into you, our bubbles could burst."

As they passed Mrs Winterberry's house, Toby had the distinct sensation someone was watching him. Did the curtain just twitch in her lounge? *Nosy so-and-so.*

When they drew level with the SMI, Toby peered

at the gates like he'd done thousands of times before. However, this time, with Bumble's tale ringing in his ears, he was even more intrigued. Was a witch really lying wounded somewhere in the grounds or imprisoned beyond those walls? Was it the girl at the window? And what was happening to her?

Toby found himself looking at everything with fresh eyes. He examined the entrance but couldn't see anything new. The building itself wasn't visible behind the thick metal gates. Then he read the sign: '*SMI – Authorised Personnel Only*'. That was strange. Toby had always thought it said: 'Solar Material Investigation'. Where on earth had he got that idea then? Was it a rumour that the SMI was set up for space exploration? What did SMI actually stand for? Although Toby couldn't see the two witches in their bubbles, he suspected they too were studying the sign.

They reached the park without incident and, directed by Willow, made their way to a small copse of trees in one corner. There were few people in the park. Good job his friends weren't playing football that afternoon.

Once they were hidden amongst the trees, Willow placed Toby in an invisible bubble as well. "Now, are you ready to begin broomstick practice?" she asked.

Toby's insides tightened. He didn't like heights at the best of times but being asked to fly on a stick the width of his wrist was beyond a joke.

The three of them stepped into the open, and

Willow placed the broom in front of her, where it settled in the air three feet off the ground. She motioned for Toby to climb astride and, reluctantly, he obeyed.

Willow held out her wand, and the broom rose gently, enough for Toby's feet to leave the ground. He wobbled but, clutching the stick with his hands and knees, managed to stay upright. It was so difficult to remain seated on the broom when it wasn't even moving. And the bubble made it worse, detaching Toby from reality.

Under Witch Willow's direction, the broom edged forward. Immediately, Toby swung round and hung swaying upside down. The blood rushed to his brain, and embarrassment filled him. He must look a complete fool hanging there, waiting for the witches to come to his rescue. Thank goodness no one else could see him. Willow lowered the broom till Toby's head touched the floor where he slithered clumsily onto the grass. Slumped on the ground, Toby lay motionless for a few seconds. He had a strong desire to run away, leaving the witches and this crazy day far, far behind.

"Never mind!" came Willow's rallying voice. "That always happens the first time. Try again!"

Sitting astride the hovering broomstick for the second time, Toby listened to Witch Willow's instructions: "Now, remember, keep your head up and your eyes focused on the direction you wish to travel. Keep your back straight but your shoulders down."

This time, as the broom flew forwards, Toby wobbled to the left. He managed to correct his balance, only to swing too far to the right, and there he was again, hanging upside down, rocking like a pendulum.

"How long does it normally take to learn to ride a broomstick?" Toby asked dubiously as he mounted the broom for the third time.

"Um, a few months," replied Willow in an apologetic tone.

"And I have an hour?!"

"Yes, but at least you're not having to learn to steer the broomstick too," she said with an encouraging nod.

After ten attempts, Toby could just about sit upright on the broom while it moved in a straight line. By this time, he was exhausted and wanted nothing more than to collapse on his sofa in front of the television.

"I'm afraid we must carry on, Toby," said Willow. "Time is pressing; we have no idea what danger Skylark may be in. Now, you need to be able to fly close enough to the SMI to see if this gun can detect Earthens as well as witches. This means you have to learn to travel up as well as forwards in order to fly over your garden hedge."

While the broom flew level with the ground, Toby remained sitting. So far so good. However, as soon as it began to rise, he panicked. Forgetting Witch Willow's instructions, he glanced down at the diminishing ground. Waves of dizziness spread through him, and he fell forwards wrapping his arms around the stick. Seeing his distress, Willow guided the broomstick around and prepared to bring Toby into land.

"Achoo!" A tremendous sneeze erupted from Bumble. She'd been standing on one foot to rest her ankle, and the force of the unexpected explosion toppled her sideways into Willow. The two of them collapsed in a heap on the ground, the Head Witch's wand flying from her grasp. The broomstick became out of control, zooming forward then spiralling into a nosedive. Toby clung on until, with a buck like a restless horse, it deposited him on top of the pile of women.

There was an ominous popping sound as his invisible bubble burst. Toby scrambled up. If anyone saw him scrabbling around on the floor with two middle-aged women, he'd never hear the last of it. Witch Willow too hurried to her feet. Brushing herself down, she soon returned to her normal unruffled composure.

With her injured ankle, Witch Bumble, however, remained on the grass as if she'd been tackled by a whole football team. As Willow reached out a hand, Barnaby peeped out of Bumble's pocket and bared his fangs.

"Bumble!" said Willow. "Control your fluttermouse."

"Well, you did squash him," Bumble pouted.

Willow withdrew her hand and left Toby to haul her companion to standing.

"Bubbling cauldrons," said Bumble, once she was on her feet. "Blasted Summer Snizzles." She ripped a purple patch from her dress and blew her nose heartily with it.

"I see your dress is still serving you well?" Willow raised one eyebrow.

"Oh yes, best thing I ever made." Bumble beamed.

Toby stared at her skirt. There was definitely a hole, but then a new purple patch grew over the gap. So he hadn't imagined the hole when she'd torn out the patch for a bandage in the attic. She hadn't taken it from a pocket. The dress had the ability to mend itself! Toby picked at the rip in his T-shirt sleeve from climbing into Mrs Winterberry's garden that morning. Shame it couldn't also regrow itself.

"Perhaps it's time we took a break," suggested Willow, glancing from Toby's tired face to Bumble's flushed cheeks.

Toby was about to agree when he heard a noise; a familiar noise which made his stomach clench. He didn't need to turn around to know who was raucously approaching.

"Aw, look! Bean's come to the park with his two nannies and their broomsticks!" jeered Boz, much to the amusement of his companions.

"Let's go," muttered Toby, moving away.

"Don't go, Toby. We want to play Bull's Eye Bean!" Whoops and caterwauls rippled through the group dressed in tracksuit bottoms and T-shirts. A few wore baseball caps, but they'd obviously decided it was too hot for their usual hoodies.

Toby continued walking, ignoring the cold eyes that bored into his back. Gritting his teeth, he waited for the clods of soil, stones, or whatever else the gang could lay its hands on, to strike. Nothing hit him. A couple of stones whizzed past and others fell short, dropping to the ground. *What was going on?* Normally at least some of the items hit his white tuft of hair. Grunts of frustration came from behind.

Toby examined the witches. To his right, Bumble seemed unaware of her surroundings, intent only on not falling over as she limped along, leaning on the broom. To his left, Willow stared innocently ahead. She saw Toby looking and gave him a small, sweet smile before returning her gaze to the front. And then he spotted it, a slight twitch of Willow's sleeve which concealed her wand.

There came a loud cry of fury. Toby couldn't resist peering over his shoulder. There, in the middle of the gang, stood Dacker: his careful styling ruined, his hair dripping with more than just the gel he'd applied that morning. The crows circling around his head had found their target. The corners of Toby's mouth twitched. Dacker's mates collapsed in guffaws, clutching their stomachs and roaring.

It was when the second serving landed on Boz that Toby, too, could contain his amusement no more. His whole body shook with silent chuckles while the two boys desperately tried to shake the mess from their hair. Toby laughed until his eyes watered and then, abruptly, he stopped. When was the last time he had laughed? Months? Years, maybe. It felt so alien. A lightness spread through Toby's body as if, for the moment at least, a weight had been lifted from his shoulders.

"I think now may be a good time to leave," said Witch Willow.

With the gang's attention still focused on Dacker and Boz, she placed herself, Bumble and Toby in invisible bubbles.

As the three of them walked towards the park exit, Toby glanced sideways at Willow. First impressions could clearly be deceptive. Beneath her self-possessed, cool exterior, there lurked a sense of humour. Somewhere behind them, Boz was still bellowing with rage. Toby smiled. For the first time since the witches' arrival, he began to see that having them around could have its benefits. *Two to Toby.*

CHAPTER ELEVEN

That evening, Toby sat eating dinner with his mum. He'd left the three witches soundproofed in the lounge. Eyeing the beef burgers he'd given them with suspicion, Willow, wand in hand, had added more food to the plates. The blue vegetable with a head like broccoli looked particularly disgusting and smelt worse, like a week-old bin of rotting cabbage.

"Sprugel," Bumble had said as Toby screwed up his nose.

He watched his mum as she ate. She must be especially tired that day – even lifting the food to her mouth was a colossal effort. Dark patches circled her eyes as she leant against the faded pink pillow. It had been ages since Toby washed her bed clothes, but it was difficult for Mum to sit out of bed, so he was more than happy to ignore this task. In the past, she would have hated lying on stale sheets. Now, she was too ill to care.

Toby had no appetite, his thoughts entirely preoccupied with stage two of Operation Witch Detector. In an hour and a half, he was supposed to fly over the back hedge on a broomstick, straight into the firing line of an unpredictable weapon. It was absurd. *What was he thinking?* Why was he helping the witches? Not that he'd ever really agreed to help – but somehow, there didn't seem to be any way to disentangle himself.

Out of the window, the giant SMI telescope, or rather gun, rotated slowly, just visible above their hedge. "Mum …" Toby attempted to sound casual. "What does the telescope do?"

"Toby," she replied wearily, "you know I can't tell you that."

"But it's been so long since you worked there. I mean, can't you even tell me what the building is like inside?"

"Why this sudden interest?"

Toby shrugged. "Just wondering."

"I might not work there anymore, but it's still top secret."

"Are they looking for planets? ... Or something else?"

No reply.

"How do you get inside?" he pushed. "Does your pass still work?"

Mum's eyebrows shot up.

He'd gone a step too far.

"Toby! Whatever you are up to, it better have nothing to do with the SMI!" Her voice was stern despite her fatigue.

"There's nothing going on, Mum."

"Toby, are you listening? This is important. I'm going to tell you something I haven't told you before," she said in an unexpectedly serious tone. "You know I receive a monthly payment and that's how we can afford to keep this house?"

Toby nodded.

"Well, the money comes from the SMI. So it's vital you don't do anything stupid. Anyone who tried to interfere in the SMI would get into a lot of trouble, but if *you* got into bother with them we could lose our money, our house. We couldn't afford to live without our SMI income." Her voice trembled.

"Don't worry, Mum; everything will be fine." Removing her empty plate from her lap, Toby helped her lie back down. He knew he should comfort her, but inside he was knotted with anger: anger at his mum for making him feel guilty, anger at the reversal of roles and always being the one who had to bear the responsibilities of an adult.

Toby sat on the edge of the bed, his feet tightly crossed and his hands screwed together. He tried to calm down and focus on making sense of what she'd just told him. "I don't get it. Why do the SMI pay you money, even though you're no longer working there?"

"They have a disability policy – if you're too ill to work, they continue to pay you."

Toby stopped himself from asking her to explain further. She wouldn't cope with any more questions.

Leaving her trapped within the same never-changing four walls, he carried the dinner plates slowly downstairs. Surely Mum's cleaning job wasn't important enough to the SMI for them to carry on paying her? And why had she felt the need to keep it a secret from him? One thing was for sure, he wouldn't tell the witches his mum had worked for the SMI, or that that's where their money came from.

Half an hour later, Toby and the three witches sat around the lounge watching the television. Willow had taken care of the washing up with a single flick of her wand. Despite being tense with anxiety, Toby had almost chuckled with glee at the ease with which she'd finished the job. If only it was always that simple. Now, however, he sat in the lounge struggling to work out what to do. He felt paralysed between the needs of his mum and those of the witches. Should he think of Mum, lying upstairs so ill in bed? Or should he think of these strangers who had elbowed their way into his life and assumed he would help?

The witches, captivated by the television, seemed oblivious to Toby's inner turmoil. Willow had insisted on watching the news, intrigued to learn more about the country. Unfortunately, the headline 'Murders in Kent' could only be heightening their fear of Earthens. As the news finished, Toby turned down the volume and cleared his throat. The witches looked at him in surprise as if awakening from a doze.

He took a deep breath and blurted out, "I'm sorry.

I can't help you."

Bumble inhaled sharply, but before she could say anything, Toby continued. "It's my mum. She's so ill. She knows something is going on and the worry makes her worse."

There was a momentary silence and then Bumble spluttered, "What about Skylark? Her life is in danger!"

"You don't know that! You don't know what's happening to her. She might be fine."

Then came Witch Hazel's quiet voice. "When Skylark's sister, Daisy, went missing two years ago, she was with two older witches. And they were in THIS area. None of them have been seen or heard from since."

The hairs stood up on the back of Toby's neck. Two years ago? His head swam. The memory surfaced again. He tried to push it away, but this time it was unstoppable. It was as if Hazel's words had burst a dam in his brain. *A woman pounding her fists against the SMI window. Mouth wide open in a silent scream.* Had that also been a witch? Two men had dragged her across the room. She had resisted, clawing at their faces, kicking out. Then something had been plunged into her arm, a syringe maybe, though it was too far away to be sure. The woman had fallen limp to the floor.

That was the last Toby had seen of her. He'd done nothing to help her and it had haunted him ever since, hidden at the back of his mind, like a monster scratching its fingernails down his door. He hadn't told anyone. Who was there to tell? Mum had only just fallen ill. He couldn't give her more things to worry about.

Toby screwed up his eyes, trying to banish the images. He'd fought to suppress the memory for so long and he needed to do so again. This was not his problem. He had to stand his ground. "I can't help you. You'll have to rescue her yourselves."

"But you know we can't! There's a witch detector!" cried Bumble. She and Toby glared at each other from either side of the lounge.

"I'm sorry, Toby," Willow's calm voice interrupted. "It seems we have been asking too much of you. Forgive us. Can I ask one favour though? And then we will leave and not trouble you again."

Toby frowned.

"Please can you continue with tonight's plan? So we can discover if the SMI gun does detect the presence of Earthens too?"

Three pairs of eyes beseeched him. The pressure was too much. Trying to push from his head the image of Mum lying so poorly in bed, Toby gave an almost imperceptible nod. "OK," he said in a barely audible voice.

CHAPTER TWELVE

8.30pm: time for stage two of Operation Witch Detector – the time Toby was dreading. He'd spent the rest of the evening gazing out of the window, listening to the clock tick. Now dusk was falling. Hopefully, it would still be light enough for him to see but dim enough to mask his movements if his bubble burst. Besides, it was Saturday, surely there wouldn't be anyone at the SMI?

Toby sat hovering on a broomstick midway down the garden with Witch Willow and Witch Bumble at his side. He shot a last furtive glance towards Mum's bedroom though even if she looked out of the window, they weren't visible in their bubbles. Under Willow's command, the broom moved forwards. Toby sat rigidly, the stick clenched between his knees and his eyes focused ahead. As the broom rose, Toby's concentration faltered and he wobbled. To avoid swinging upside down, he lay forwards and flew over the hedge, clearing it only by centimetres. He passed the metre of No-man's-land and the high barbed wire fence.

Onwards the broom flew with its amateur passenger. Warily, Toby lifted his head. Although he'd flown quite a few metres into the SMI enclosure, the gun on top of the building showed no signs of detecting him. This must be far enough. Surely Willow wouldn't be able to see him if he went much further? He gritted his teeth, praying she would turn the broom around and fly him back to safety. Unfortunately, quite the opposite happened. The broomstick gave a sudden jerk, shot forwards and dumped Toby onto the roof of the SMI before flopping down beside him.

Toby scrabbled to a sitting position. What had happened? Why had Willow done that? He studied the air – had his bubble burst? No, a slight haziness hung around him: he was still invisible. *Phew.* So here he was, in the SMI grounds. How many hundreds of times had he wished he could see beyond the SMI gates? Yet now that he was inside, he had no desire to be there at all. Anger flooded through him. *Stupid witches!* All he'd done to help and now, thanks to them, he was going to get into big trouble. He inhaled deeply, trying to calm his fury. This was not the time. He needed to concentrate on how on earth he was going to get out of this mess.

Toby examined his surroundings. The barbed wire fence bordered the entire perimeter of the grounds, and beyond that grew the thick hedge that skirted his garden. A drive led from the imposing metal gates to the main door. To one side lay a small car park, in which two cars were still parked in spite of the late hour. Grass covered the rest of the compound. The building itself resembled a square horseshoe. Thankfully, Toby had landed at one end, a safe distance from the large gun in the middle which continued slowly circling the sky. It had shown no sign of noticing Toby's presence.

Whilst most of the building was two stories high, Toby sat above the main door which was only one storey from the ground. Unfortunately, it was still too high for him to jump. He peered over the side through the dimming light to see if it was possible to step onto a windowsill. To his surprise, there appeared to be no windows below him at all. Was the work of the SMI so secretive that they couldn't even have windows near ground level?

The roof was dotted with small skylights. A few metres away one was open and light spilled out. Voices drifted through. Straining to hear, Toby crawled closer. The flat roof of the building was rough, and he winced with pain as gravel dug into his palms and knees. Through the skylight, a man sat at a desk bearing the nameplate 'Director, Society of Magical Investigation'. *So that was what 'SMI' stood for!* It didn't mean Solar Material Investigation at all. The witches were right – it *was* set up to find them!

"So have you found out where the witches live?" the Director asked a person in a part of the room Toby couldn't see.

"She's still refusing to talk," replied a male voice that sounded like Dacker's dad.

"And how are the experiments going?"

"We're doing blood tests. Initial results are proving interesting. Like previous experiments, it does appear that witches have components in their blood not present in humans."

"And do you think we'll discover how their magic works this time?" said the Director. "The sooner we know how to recreate it, the sooner we'll have a power to match theirs. Who knows what they might do." As he talked, he twiddled a small silver stick between his fingers.

"It's too early to say. We'll continue the examination of her blood for a couple more days and then ..." The man paused as if searching for the correct words.

"And then you will begin the more invasive investigations," finished the Director.

The words sent a chill shuddering through Toby's body.

"And is the young witch cooperating?" the Director continued.

"She's a wilful type, but she has no choice."

Bumble had been telling the truth. The SMI did have Skylark! Whatever fate awaited her, it sounded disturbing to say the least.

Toby shifted position on the sharp gravel and, to his horror, some small stones scuttled through the skylight. Instantly, the men stopped talking. Toby drew back before remembering he was invisible. He held his breath, his heart pounding in his chest. After several long seconds, the silence was broken by a bird squawking nearby.

"Pesky crows!" The Director shut the skylight, and Toby could hear no more.

He retreated to the spot where he'd landed. Maybe he could manoeuvre himself onto the ground using the broomstick? Hmm, he'd probably break both legs. A familiar noise made him look up. Through the gloom, the SMI gates creaked open. A car glided through and zipped up to the main entrance below Toby. A woman swiped her card and disappeared inside. There was no time to reflect. The gates were already starting to close.

Toby clambered down from the roof onto the car. It was a larger drop than he'd anticipated and he landed with a loud thud, his bubble bursting on impact. He slithered off the side of the car and, broom in hand, began racing up the drive. The gates inched nearer together. On Toby ran. He *had* to get out. He was no longer invisible. If he didn't make it, he'd be trapped in the SMI enclosure with nowhere to hide.

Toby ran until he felt his lungs would burst. He might be fast, but the drive was long. The gates edged further together. They were going to close and he was still several metres away. Toby watched his one chance of escape fade from view. With a spurt and just centimetres to spare, he squeezed through the gates. They clanged shut behind him, sealing the SMI and its secrets beyond high walls once again.

Toby gasped for air, his chest heaving. As his breathing slowed, relief flooded his body. Thank heavens he'd not been caught trespassing. When fully recovered, he strode in the direction of his house, a furious glint in his eye.

He entered his back garden to find Witch Willow and Witch Bumble still standing there, fraught expressions on their faces. "Toby!" cried the latter, throwing her arms up in the air. "Thank the stars!"

He glared at them and stalked through the door. Hurrying after him, the witches removed their bubbles and soundproofed the kitchen.

"Toby, I'm so sorry," said Willow. "I've never operated someone else's broom before. As soon as you went out of sight I lost control."

Toby remained silent.

"Are you alright?" prompted Willow. "Did anything happen?"

"I'm fine," he muttered. "And the SMI gun did not detect me."

"Thank you, Toby. We are extremely grateful for your help. I have one final request; please will you permit us to stay till the morning? Flying visibility is poor at night. But don't worry, by the time you wake we'll be gone, and you will never see or hear from us again."

CHAPTER THIRTEEN

Toby lay in bed, tossing and turning, but sleep wouldn't come. His mind spun with everything he'd seen and heard that day, like a colourful carousel that wouldn't stop twirling. Just when the ride seemed to be slowing, more images crowded in from every side, and the merry-go-round would begin again.

Voices plagued him.

There were his mum's tired anxious tones: 'Whatever you're up to, it better have nothing to do with the SMI ... if you got into bother with them, we could lose our money, our house ...'

Followed by the ominous words of the SMI Director: 'And then you will begin the more invasive investigations ...'

And finally Witch Willow's voice: 'By the time you wake, we will be gone, and you will never see or hear from us again.'

They echoed in his ears over and over until he felt he would go crazy. Whom should he help? Should he think of Mum, so poorly? And what about his own needs? He certainly didn't fancy getting into any trouble, let alone losing their income. Or should he think of Skylark, a young witch he'd never met who faced … well what exactly? He shuddered to imagine. Two years ago, he'd done nothing. Was this his chance to make amends? And stop the memory that haunted him?

And why did Willow's words bother him so much? The witches were leaving – wasn't that what he wanted? And yet, the idea left him cold. He'd discovered so much in the past twenty-four hours, it would be impossible to forget about it. His life would never be the same again.

All these thoughts burrowed into his core, like termites gnawing on wood.

Around midnight, Toby gave up on sleep and sat up. For several seconds, he gazed at the shadows in his room, steeling himself for the decision he was about to make. Then he let out a sigh. He knew what he had to do.

Tiptoeing downstairs, Toby stepped over the third and fifth steps which always creaked. He pushed open the lounge door and peered inside. A figure stirred in the dark and switched on a lamp. Its dim glow illuminated Witch Willow sitting in a magically lengthened armchair and regarding Toby with a quizzical expression. He closed the lounge door softly before drawing up a stool beside her.

Witch Bumble lay sprawled on her back on the sofa, her mouth gaping and one arm hanging over the edge. Every few seconds she emitted a rasping, bone-rattling snore. A sleeping Witch Hazel occupied the other elongated armchair, her quiet breathing periodically accompanied by a small popping sound on an out-breath.

Toby sat staring ahead without speaking and Witch Willow waited without prompting. Finally, he cleared his throat. "SMI stands for 'Society of Magical Investigation'. I saw it through a window in the building."

"As I suspected," replied Willow gravely.

"They do have Skylark. I overheard the Director talking. They are doing blood tests and in a couple of days they plan to begin ..." Toby swallowed, "... the more invasive investigations."

Willow pursed her lips, but her face remained as impassive as ever. "I see."

"What do you think will happen to her?"

"I dread to imagine. I suspect the SMI is trying to discover how our magic works, with the objective of recreating it for themselves. They'll never succeed of course. A witch's magic is unique to herself; it runs through her veins like a silver strand in her blood and works only in conjunction with her individually made wand."

"What do you plan to do?"

"I've no idea."

There was silence.

"If I ... I mean, an Earthen," Toby hastily

corrected himself, "were to rescue Skylark, how do you assume they'd go about it?"

"We have some magical tools that can help in that matter. A secret-seeker, for example, which enables the user to pass through locked doors." Willow looked into his eyes. "Why don't you come to Little Witchery with us tomorrow?"

"Little Witchery? Up in the sky?" spluttered Toby.

"Yes, there are some things I'd like to show you which might, well, help you to make a decision."

"I'm not making any promises."

"I know. We'll leave at 10am with or without you."

CHAPTER FOURTEEN

The kitchen clock gave a loud tick as Toby closed the lounge door behind him; both hands had hit the twelve. It was midnight. *It was midnight*! He was supposed to be meeting Dacker and Boz at the park. How could he have forgotten?

Toby hesitated, he didn't have to go. But no, he must. He couldn't risk anyone else seeing that video, it being on some website for the whole world to watch, for someone to take him away. Would he get it back tonight? Somehow he felt it might not be that simple.

He was tiptoeing out of the door when Willow peered into the kitchen. "Where are you going?" she whispered.

"Nowhere."

"Mmm."

"It's nothing. It's not important." Toby shut the door before she could ask any more questions.

Above his garden, a small creature flitted in the air. Was that a bird? At night? Or was it Bumble's bat? Toby shielded his head and hurried down his drive.

At the corner of Fir Tree Close, he paused, half

expecting Jazz to be there again. But she wasn't. Well, he didn't want her help anyway, did he?

It was already five past twelve. He ran, reducing his jog to a walk when he reached the park; he didn't want Dacker and Boz to realise how bothered he was. They'd know he was worried though. They'd guess he'd do anything to prevent the video being seen.

"You're late," hissed Dacker. He sidled towards Toby and circled him with penetrating eyes, a snake sizing up its prey.

Toby could practically spot a forked tongue flicker between his lips. Dacker had been made a fool of at the park that afternoon; clearly he was still fuming. There was a stronger air of hostility about him tonight. Toby dug his nails into his palm.

Dacker held out his hand to Boz who passed him a large jar. It glinted in the light from the street lamp, and inside, two earthworms coiled themselves into knots. Dacker passed the jar to Toby.

"Hungry?" Boz sneered.

"Eat them," said Dacker.

The worms slithered around the slippery glass. Toby hesitated; he wasn't sure he could do this. He gazed across the park. A couple who'd had too much to drink were swaying past, giggling and leaning on each other for support. The pair peered at the three figures by the swings, then carried on and were soon out of sight.

"Unless you'd rather we showed …" Boz taunted.

101

"I'll do it." Toby knew he had no choice. "But that'll be the end. You'll destroy the video?"

Gingerly, he put his hand into the jar and pulled out a writhing worm. He lifted it to his lips. Don't think about it! Don't think. Take a bite as soon as it's in your mouth to stop it wriggling.

Boz and Dacker held their breath and shuddered. But as the worm touched Toby's tongue, a strange thing happened: the worm lay still. And stranger yet, when Toby bit down, there was no iron tang of blood. Instead, a sweet syrup filled his mouth. It was delicious!

"Ugh!" cried Boz.

Toby pretended to grimace; he had to make them believe he was doing what they wanted. Boz strutted around, grinning from ear to ear, the feeling of power gone to his head.

Toby picked up the next worm, this one covered in earth. As he raised it, a jangling sound came from behind. He froze, the worm dangling in mid-air.

A man holding a torch was unlocking the park gates. "What do ya think you're playing at? The gate is locked for a reason, ya know!"

Dacker grabbed Toby's arm. "Tomorrow night."

"What? Wait. I thought that was the end of it?"

"There's a small job we need doing. 84 Lewis Road. Midnight tomorrow. Be there."

"Mr. McClean's house," sniggered Boz.

Toby gaped. *Mr. McClean's house?* The maths

teacher? That sounded bad. That sounded a whole lot worse than eating worms. There was no time to reply, the night watchman was striding towards them. Toby wanted to hurl the jar so it shattered at Dacker's feet. But who knew how he'd retaliate? Dropping it onto the woodchips where he stood, Toby burst into a run.

"Watch it!" he heard Dacker yell as Boz collided with him and almost knocked him over.

Toby suppressed a smile. He sprinted into the gloomy park. As his feet pounded the earth, his spirits lifted. Running always did this to him. He was so fast, he flew with the wind. He missed his football matches: the ball at his feet, facing the goalkeeper and feeling confident he would score.

Toby looked back, sure the two boys wouldn't be able to keep up. Dacker wasn't a bad runner, yet he was still some way behind, his outline silhouetted in the light from the distant lamp post. Further away, the watchman was clinging onto Boz's arm. The man was taller, but he was no match for twelve-year-old Boz in build. How big would the boy be when he reached adult size? With his free hand, Boz swiped the man across the face. He stumbled, and Boz started running, striding clumsily in his stomping gait.

For once, the dark didn't bother Toby. The danger was behind, not in front. And he was far away from it now. At the other side of the park, Toby slowed to a trot. There was a stream around here somewhere, he didn't want to go charging headfirst into it. He strained to see in the night. He could use the light from his phone screen, but then he'd show Dacker and Boz where he was. Now, where was the bridge which led to the park's back entrance? He groped in front and his fingers grasped the handrail.

Toby edged forwards. No one went this way anymore and the bridge was falling apart. The wooden planks wobbled under his feet and the railings rattled in their foundations. It wasn't a big drop to the stream, but he didn't fancy getting wet and muddy. Toby eased himself across the bridge. As he neared the other bank, his right foot stepped into thin air. He grabbed the handrail, narrowly avoiding the plunge into the murky depths below. Heart thumping at the shock, Toby heaved himself backwards and peered down. It was so dark! There was definitely a plank missing, but he couldn't make out where the gap ended. Trusting to luck, he launched himself across the hole. The plank he landed on cracked loudly, and he leapt onto the next one. Turning round, he kicked at the rotten wood. It cracked some more.

Toby glanced at the rest of the park. The watchman had given up catching the boys and was relocking the gate at the far side. There was no sign of Dacker and Boz. They'd been swallowed by the gloom. Well, at least they wouldn't be able to see Toby either. Still, he didn't have time to waste, they'd catch up soon. He stamped hard on the plank. With a sad creak, it splintered into pieces and vanished into the stream. *Perfect.* The gap was now too wide for them to jump.

Toby sprang off the bridge onto the far bank and clambered over the old entrance gate. He was joining the next street when he heard the satisfying sound of a loud splash, followed by an angry yell. *Three to Toby.*

When he was sure he wasn't being followed, Toby stopped running. It had been a crazy day, so much had happened. He should be fast asleep; it was one in the morning. Each footstep felt heavy, but his mind still raced. Why on earth had the worms tasted so nice? Toby had his suspicions. And why did Dacker and Boz want to meet him at Mr McClean's house? Boz hated maths. And he hated the maths teacher even more. What were they going to make Toby do?

He was halfway home when the whirring of bicycle wheels made his heart miss a beat. Dacker and Boz! They'd caught up with him. Toby spun round to face them … and was met with Roger and Jazz. They jumped off their bikes, and Jazz gave an awkward smile.

"Umm … we couldn't see what they were doing, but when the watchman came along, we thought it might be best to tell him there was someone in the park. Get them off your back …" She bit her lip.

Toby paused before giving a small nod. "Thanks."

Jazz let out a sigh of relief. "Oh good. We weren't sure what was best."

"What did they want, mate?" Roger asked.

Toby shook his head. Silence fell as the three of them walked along the pavement; the creaking of the bicycle chains the only sound.

"Dacker fell in the stream," said Toby suddenly.

"In the stream?" cried Jazz. "I wish I'd been there!"

"Yeah, I didn't see, but I heard the splash. And the yell. He didn't sound too happy."

Roger snorted. "I hope Boz landed on top of him."

Jazz let out a peal of laughter and Toby grinned. It felt good to be the three of them. How long had it been since they had hung out together? Too long.

"Let us know, right, if Tweedledum and Tweedledee want you to do anything else," Roger said as they reached Toby's road.

"Um," Toby began. "They want me to meet them tomorrow night actually. At Mr McClean's house."

Roger sucked in a sharp breath. "They're gonna get you into serious trouble. Don't go."

"I have to. I can't explain why, but I don't have any choice."

"Then we'll come with you," replied Jazz.

Toby hesitated. "Alright … Thanks."

"Well, we'd better get home," said Roger. "Cross your fingers I sneak in without being caught. Lucas woke when I was leaving and wanted to come."

"What did you say?" asked Toby. Sharing a bedroom with your brother sounded fun, but Roger hated it.

"Told him it was witching hour and if he got up he'd be turned into a mouse."

Toby forced a smile. Just a day ago, he too would've found the notion of witches completely bonkers.

Jazz and Roger jumped on their bikes and pedalled off into the night.

Toby watched after them, a small glow in his heart. The thought of having backup next time he met Dacker and Boz made everything seem a little easier.

Passing the gates of the SMI, Dacker's words from the previous night surfaced in Toby's brain. What had he said? Something about leaving the video camera at the SMI for 'safekeeping'. So was it in there now? The germ of an idea took root. If Toby did help the witches, if he did find a way to rescue Skylark, then might he be able to find the camera as well? Toby made a decision. He would go to Little Witchery in the morning and see what the witches had in mind. Perhaps he would break into the SMI for them, if it meant he could get his hands on that video. It would be better than meeting up with Dacker and Boz at Mr McClean's house. It was certainly worth considering.

CHAPTER FIFTEEN

"But what about the oath?" exclaimed Bumble the next morning, as the three witches and Toby sat around the kitchen table.

Willow turned to Toby. "You understand that no Earthen has ever been inside Little Witchery before? Or even known of its existence? It's always been of utmost importance for the safety of the wyline clan to keep its location a secret. To this end, every witchette must pledge an oath upon their life."

Willow turned back to Bumble. "Remind yourself of the oath, Bumble?"

"I, Witch Bumble, of pure witch blood," Bumble muttered, "vow never to reveal the location of Little Witchery for misintent or misdeed. This oath I swear upon my life."

"And so, are we revealing the location to Toby for misintent or misdeed?"

"No ... but ..."

"Skylark is in serious danger. If Toby is to help us, I believe there are certain things in our town which would be beneficial for him to see. So, are we ready to depart?"

"I'll stay here and look after Toby's mother," chirped up Witch Hazel.

Toby flinched. "She'll be fine. She thinks I'm spending the day with Roger. I've left lunch by her bed, like on school days, and apart from that she just needs quiet so she can rest."

Witch Hazel, however, was not to be deterred. "I insist! I'm a Protector: I care for sick witches in our hospital." There was a hint of pride in her soft voice.

"Well, don't bother my mum," Toby warned. "I'll be home in time to cook her dinner."

In the garden, the two witches mounted their broomsticks. Bumble's dress flowed out over her broom and there was no space for passengers.

"Climb on then!" cried Willow, patting the wood behind her.

With a groan, Toby clambered aboard. Waves of nausea swam over him at the thought of the journey ahead. He could hardly stay on the broom when he was a few metres off the ground, how would he survive hundreds of metres high? And of course, 'survive' was the operable word; if he were to fall ... well it didn't bear imagining.

"Ready for flight?" Willow turned to Bumble. "Take to the air!" She rose upwards. "Hold on tight!" she called to Toby as they left his garden, taking care to avoid the SMI and its rotating witch detector.

Toby's polite grasp on Willow's cloak soon

became a firm grip and, at times, a desperate clutch around her waist. Higher and higher they surged, with Bumble flying a few metres behind. Glancing downwards, Toby gaped at the scene below. He'd never flown in an aeroplane, never seen how the countryside spread out below: a hotchpotch of handkerchief-sized fields, with tiny houses and ant-like cars crawling along the roads. Looking down, however, made Toby's perch on the broomstick even more precarious and he wobbled violently. *Bad idea.* He tried closing his eyes, but this made him lose all track of which way was up. There was nothing for it but to stare straight ahead and avoid thinking of the hundreds of feet stretching beneath him.

The minutes passed interminably, broken only by the occasional buffeting of Toby's face by Willow's orange curls as they billowed behind her. It was like being hit in the mouth with a bristly doormat. Toby shivered. It was chilly at this height. He should have worn a jumper. After an endless hour, Willow shouted something, but the words were whipped away in the wind. The air surrounding them grew darker and denser and they flew through some sort of tunnel. Then they passed through a hole and entered a room not much larger than Toby's lounge. The ceiling stretched high above them with ornate carvings decorating the corners.

The broom came to a stop and hovered near the floor where Willow dismounted gracefully.

Attempting to do the same, Toby jumped down, but his legs had turned to jelly and almost gave way beneath him. He staggered forwards a few steps before bumping into a wall and slumping against it. It was Bumble's landing, however, which was the most spectacular. With one leg out of action, she skidded to a halt in a series of kangaroo-hops, narrowly missing the sentry, and fell to the floor in a heap. Although her ankle was no longer swollen, it had turned an interesting shade of purple and she massaged it dolefully before swaying to her feet. As previously agreed, Willow and Bumble removed their bubbles whilst leaving Toby invisible. '*Few members of the community know about Skylark's capture,*' Willow had explained. '*No need to cause alarm with the arrival of a male Earthen.*'

At the appearance of the Head Witch, the sentry gave a small bow before inserting her wand into a tiny, imperceptible hole in the wall. Cogs whirred into life and at one end of the room, towering wooden doors swung open. Light spilled through the archway into the gloomy room.

"Wait," whispered Willow.

Either side of the door sat a grey stone gargoyle, hunched on its hind legs. They faced each other with grotesque expressions and evil grins. Dark stubby wings grew out of their backs and horns protruded from their heads. All at once, a jet of yellow light flared out of one of their mouths and hit the wall. Toby

111

jumped in shock. Then the other gargoyle fired a shot. It struck the opposite wall, leaving a smouldering dent amongst a myriad of other scorched marks. Willow started to count:

One, two
Shots through
Three, four
And some more
Five, six
In the mix
Seven, eight
Still to wait

The shots streamed in front of the door at different angles, sometimes horizontal, sometimes diagonal, and with no discernible rhythm. There was no way anyone could get through.

Nine, ten
Time to RUN!!

Willow and Bumble raced past the gargoyles and through the archway. Toby darted after them. He was just in time as the doors slammed shut behind them. And there they stood, on the edge of Little Witchery.

CHAPTER SIXTEEN

Toby gaped wide-eyed at the scene before him, the sound of hustle and bustle filling his ears. They were in a giant transparent dome. Winding roads and buildings of all shapes, sizes and colours stretched into the distance. He inhaled deeply. The air smelt faintly of bonfire smoke, of mystery … of magic? Above, witches flew here and there in an orderly fashion. A traffic system floated in the sky, with signs suspended at intervals.

Absorbed in looking around, Toby could have stayed for hours, but Willow was already striding across a small green. Yellow flowers lining the grass, strained towards them. Three heads sprouted from each stalk and puffed out clouds of white gas in their direction.

"Don't breathe! Cover your mouth and nose. And move! QUICKLY." Willow placed her cloak sleeve over her face.

"What were *they*?" asked Toby, once they had left the flowers behind.

"They detect the presence of any strangers who

enter Little Witchery. That gas would knock you out for a day."

"If you can get past Howler and Growler first," chuckled Bumble.

Willow raised an eyebrow. "You've given our stone guards names?"

"Of course!" said Bumble.

Toby shuddered. First the gargoyles and now the flowers. He needed to stay alert.

"The town has grown since its early days," whispered Willow as they approached a row of houses, "but we still only have a few hundred inhabitants."

Turning down the first street, a wave of panic rippled through Toby. Here he was, in a strange land, in the midst of a small army of powerful magical beings whom he still wasn't sure he could trust. The further he ventured, the more trapped he would become. Yet as he walked down the street, his fear subsided in his marvel at the houses around him. They were like nothing Toby had ever seen before. Most were round, not very large and some even boasted a turret or two. But it was the uniqueness of each home that was so striking. Every dwelling seemed to have its own character, its own colour, as if it hummed with life.

They came to a cheery residence with curved sides, every shade of the rainbow. Rooms stuck off at various angles, and windows had been added in a clumsy fashion.

"My house," Bumble pointed out proudly. Her words were unnecessary; the building resembled her to a tee.

The door swung open and out shot a dog. At least, it looked like a dog (a Golden Retriever to be exact), but then it unfurled its wings and flew around Bumble's head with excited woofs.

"Get down!" laughed Bumble as the animal tried desperately to lick her face. "My Golden Retrieagle," she whispered to Toby, beaming. She ruffled its ears. "I'm sorry, you have to stay here."

With drooping ears and tail, the bird-dog sat and watched them as they continued on their way.

At the side of the road, they came to a field in which a number of witches were kneeling down amongst rows of strange-looking plants.

"Every wyline member of working age plays a role in the community," explained Willow. "Up above, you can see the Bubble Patrol – witches whose job it is to reinforce the town's invisible bubble."

A number of witches on broomsticks, so high they seemed tiny, were dotted around the inside of the dome.

"And these witches here cultivate our fresh vegetables," continued the Head Witch. "We do create our food magically too, but it's not nearly as sustaining."

"Nimnucket, sprugel." Bumble pointed out various vegetables.

At the end of the field, two witches in silver uniforms were talking to a wildly gesticulating woman.

"She stole my prize sprugel!" she cried.

"I never laid a finger on it! Now get me down from here." A witch hung upside down from a tree, her foot ensnared by a knot of twisted twigs.

Willow sighed. "Good day, Silver Keepers. Is there a problem?"

They saluted. "Good day, Witch Willow. Just a minor dispute."

"Well, I'll leave it in your capable hands." Willow turned to the owner of the missing vegetable. "But really, Witch Green, stolen sprugel or non-stolen sprugel, magic should not be used against a fellow witch. You know that."

Willow walked away before calling back, "And if someone would kindly remove Witch Waffle from the tree, I'm sure she's been there long enough."

As they left the field, a shrill whistle blew. The workers, without even looking up from the vegetables, pointed their wands upwards. Small brightly striped umbrellas sprouted from their caps as if the witches were trees growing branches.

"Watering time," said Bumble.

Large droplets of rain fell on the field while the witches, dry under their umbrellas, continued weeding and digging unperturbed.

Further on, Bumble pulled a purple fruit from a

nearby bush. "Tibtab?" She held it out to her right.

"I'm behind you!" hissed Toby.

Jumping in surprise, Bumble spun round and thrust the object forwards. Toby's bubble burst with a pop. Without a moment's hesitation, Willow resurrected it. The tibtab was the size of a ping-pong ball but shaped like a teardrop with a rough purple skin.

Plucking another from the bush, Bumble peeled apart the pointed end, held the opening to her mouth and squeezed the fleshy part. A jet of purple liquid squirted out. "Mmmm! Delicious!" She smacked her lips together.

She'd said the same about the pondweed water, and that had looked and smelt disgusting. Still, Toby was thirsty, so he peeled open the tibtab and sniffed the contents. It smelt lovely! He held it to his lips and squeezed. A rich berrylike syrup filled his mouth and trickled soothingly down his throat. Delicious indeed! It actually tasted rather familiar. What did it remind him of? Some sort of berry? No ... A fizzy drink? No … And then it hit him. The worms! The worms Dacker had made him eat in the park last night. It tasted exactly the same. Toby knew it. Willow had followed him to the park last night. She had intervened, just as she had when Dacker's gang was playing Bull's Eye Bean earlier in the day. Toby tried to catch her eye, but she was already moving on.

A short sharp siren blared throughout the town.

Toby stopped in alarm but the two witches continued walking.

"Only a small bubble intrusion." Bumble waved at the sky.

The witches tending to the dome flew swiftly till they disappeared from sight behind a tall building.

"I wonder what it will be today," chuckled Bumble. "Last Wednesday a flock of cravens got their beaks stuck in the bubble's outer layer."

"Cravens?" Toby frowned.

"You know, those big black birds."

"Oh, you mean ravens. Or crows."

"No, cravens," replied Bumble adamantly.

Toby bit his lip, arguing with her wasn't worth the effort.

A couple of streets later, Willow stopped outside an elegant-looking house which shimmered in varying shades of blue. "This is where Skylark and her mother live."

"My sister!" added Bumble with a fond expression.

Willow's knock at the door was answered with a quiet 'come in', and Toby followed the two witches into a small room. A woman sat curled up on the sofa, her eyes red and swollen; evidently she'd been told of her daughter's capture. Bumble rushed over to hold her and stroke the chestnut hair which matched her own. There was no other resemblance between them. Skylark's mother was slimmer and smarter in appearance, but Bumble seemed to give comfort as she wrapped her sister in her arms.

"Witch Wing, as you know, your daughter has been taken prisoner by an Earthen organisation," said Willow. "We know, too, that they have invented a witch detector, so any witch who approaches the building where Skylark is being held will be struck down." Witch Wing sobbed, her shoulders shaking, as Willow pressed on. "Now, I have with me, a male Earthen who may be willing to help rescue Skylark. You do understand that doing so would put him at great risk?"

Bumble's sister quietened as Willow removed Toby's invisible cover. It was good to be free of the bubble which had been making Toby increasingly spaced out as time went on, but he felt resentful at being produced like a rabbit from a hat. As he stood there in awkward silence, Witch Wing stared and shrank into the sofa. Despite Toby's wariness of this strange land, the witch appeared the more frightened one.

"Now, is there anything you can tell Toby about Skylark which might be of use to him?" Willow asked.

"Please help her. It's not her fault! She *is* headstrong. She shouldn't have gone out by herself, but I know she would have been looking for Daisy." Witch Wing gave a gulp, and her handkerchief flew to her face and dabbed her eyes.

"Do you have a picture of your daughter to show

Toby?" prompted Willow.

Wing attempted to compose herself. "I think the most recent picture of her hangs in her bedroom," she whispered after a few moments' consideration.

As Bumble turned for the stairs, she put her nose in the air and sniffed. "Do I smell Morph Munchies?"

"I made some this morning, for when Daisy and Skylark get home. They do love them."

"Of course." Bumble gave a sad smile.

A plate piled high with biscuits lifted from the kitchen counter and soared over to Bumble.

"Oh no, I really shouldn't." She held up her hands in protest.

The plate nudged her on the arm.

"Well, if you insist." Bumble bit into a biscuit, showering the floor with crumbs.

The plate glided to Willow, but she waved it away, so it moved onto Toby. Apart from the tibtab, he hadn't eaten anything since breakfast, and that had been hours ago. The biscuits rose until they were hovering right under his nose. A heavenly aroma filled Toby's nostrils. He picked one and took a bite. It was warm and crumbly, and a gooey liquid oozed from the centre.

"Mmm. Moonberry," Bumble smacked her lips together.

Moonberry? It tasted of chocolate and cherries to him.

Toby was wiping his hands when Bumble started

clutching her nose. "Oh no! I got the …" Her next words were muffled as a black glossy beak grew out of her face.

"You got the craven!" cried Wing. "Daisy will be disappointed she missed seeing Aunty Bumble with a beak."

"Squawk!" said Bumble.

Toby's eyebrows shot up so high they disappeared into his hairline. The witches, however, appeared unfazed. The bottom of Toby's spine itched, and he went to scratch it. A lump was growing there. A lump, that rapidly became a bushy yellow tail. *What the …?* Toby bent his body in half trying to see behind him. *Oh great, just brilliant.* He agreed to come to Little Witchery, to help the witches, and they gave him a tail? Bull's Eye Bean was going to get a whole lot worse when school started again.

The tail wagged of its own accord, and Toby's whole backside wagged too.

Bumble pointed her finger at him. "Squawk!" Her tummy shook with mirth.

"Really," said Willow with exasperation, "we didn't bring Toby here to turn him into a dog. Witch Wing, you mentioned you had a picture of Skylark?"

"Yes, this way." Bumble's sister headed for the stairs.

"Don't panic." Willow put a hand on Toby's shoulder. "The effects of Morph Munchies don't last long."

Toby followed the witches up a crooked, circular staircase, the wooden steps creaking with every wag of his tail. To his great relief, by the time they reached the top, he and Bumble were already returning to normal. The staircase led to three doors, one of which Witch Wing pushed open. *Skylark's room.* It emitted such a dazzling ice blue, it took Toby's breath away. And, before he looked at the picture on the wall, he knew Skylark would be beautiful. She was: blonde hair, sparkling blue eyes and high cheekbones. Toby's heart gave a little thump. Was this the girl he'd seen at the SMI window the other night? She'd been too far away to be certain, but she'd definitely had blonde hair, it had shone in the light from the room.

"Do you have a smaller version of this?" he asked. "I mean," he continued quickly, blushing, "if I am to recognize Skylark in the SMI, it might help if I had a picture of her with me …" He trailed off.

Willow suppressed a smile.

"Here! I have one." Bumble pulled a piece of paper from her cloak, and Toby thrust it into his pocket.

As he turned to leave the room, a smaller portrait on Skylark's bedside table caught his attention. Another picture of a girl with golden hair. The eyes glimmered blue like Skylark's, but they were different, gentler.

"That's Daisy," whispered Wing. "I hear Skylark up here sometimes talking away to the picture, telling her sister she'll find her." A tear rolled down her cheek and fell to the floor.

"She's a shy little thing is Daisy," said Bumble. "But you should have seen her with Skylark; her petals unfurled like a flower in sunshine. I could listen to the two of them giggling for hours."

Witch Wing gave another muffled sob.

"We'll get them back, don't you worry." Bumble put her arm around her sister. "We'll get them back."

Toby looked away. Across the landing, a second bedroom door stood ajar. It bore a piece of paper with the word 'Daisy' in wonky lettering. A faint yellow light pulsed within; it seemed to grow dimmer even as Toby watched.

CHAPTER SEVENTEEN

From Skylark's house, Willow, Bumble and Toby continued deeper into Little Witchery. Toby couldn't stop thinking about the beautiful witch. Every so often he checked her picture was still in his pocket. Now and then, they passed witches who would always incline their heads politely to Willow, apart, that is, from a witch with long flowing hair as black as her cloak.

"Witch Willow," she said, her lips curling at the edges.

"Witch Ebonia." Willow's tone was even, but the tension in the air was palpable.

Goosebumps formed on Toby's arms. He was glad he was invisible.

"Is it true Skylark has been captured?" said Ebonia.

"Just a rumour. And I trust you'll keep it to yourself. We don't want the whole clan to panic unnecessarily." Willow didn't break her stride, but Ebonia, with height and leg length to match the Head Witch, kept pace.

"I believe it is time we took action, show Earthens

what we are capable of."

"You know where I stand on that one. Fighting back is not the solution," replied Willow.

"Then you leave me no choice," said Ebonia. "I hereby raise a challenge to your leadership."

Bumble gasped. Willow stopped and turned to face Ebonia. "You have the twenty signatories?"

Ebonia, her startling green eyes never wavering, handed Willow a piece of paper. "I'm calling for a vote tomorrow evening."

Tight-lipped, Willow scanned the paper; the words *'In support of Witch Ebonia for Head Witch'* embossed in gold at the top.

"Very well, I will see you there." Willow walked off without a backward glance.

"Flapping fluttermice!" cried Bumble as soon as Ebonia was out of earshot. "This is terrible. Terrible!"

"What's she going to do?" asked Toby.

"Do not worry," said Willow. "Witch Ebonia will not have the majority. Few of the clan believe war is the way forward. Our wyline ancestors already suffered too much at the hands of Earthens."

"But …" Bumble began.

"I will not hear another word of this," replied Willow sharply.

Bumble clamped her mouth shut and trailed behind, wringing her hands. Toby chewed the inside of his cheek. *Ebonia wanted to go to war against Earthens?* What would happen if she beat Willow?

Soon, a gothic-styled building came into view. It was small yet imposing with dark stone and a steeple at each end. The words '*The Silver Academy for Witchettes*' were inscribed above the entrance. In a yard attached to the building, six young witches balanced on broomsticks. Well, five balanced, the sixth hung upside down swaying from side to side, flustered and red-faced.

"No, no!" The teacher said with an air of impatience. "Eyes up, shoulders down!"

Toby threw the girl a sympathetic look; he knew just how she must be feeling.

They came to a square at the heart of the town. In the centre, water danced in a stone fountain. Spouts twisted and turned, downwards and upwards, defying gravity. The place was empty, save for a couple of older witches sitting on benches and watching the world go by.

"Waiting for the midday meal already," chuckled Bumble.

Along the right-hand side stood a row of shops: '*Conifer's Corner*', '*The Bobbin*'. They had much in common with the witches' houses – small, round and full of character. On the left, a large building ran the whole length of the square. Willow strode towards it. Inside, long trestle tables lined the hall and a vaulted ceiling stretched high above. Plates whizzed through the air directed by a witch who stood muttering and waving her wand. It all looked so complicated, surely some would crash together? Yet, each piece of crockery managed to end up neatly in its place on a table. Toby watched in awe.

The smell of cooked vegetables wafted towards them. "Mmm, nimnucket stew," said Bumble. "This is where I work." She gazed around with satisfaction. "Helping to prepare the food for the whole community."

Willow shepherded them to the far end of the hall, keeping close to the wall to avoid the flying plates. She led them along a corridor past several doors before entering the final one. Inside, she approached her secretary's desk. "Witch Ebonia has put forward a bid for Head Witch. I'll need you to start working on my campaign right away."

"Oh my. When is the vote?"

"Tomorrow evening."

The secretary's mouth fell open. "Tomorrow evening? So soon! We'll get started immediately."

"I'm afraid I won't be able to help today. I have a more pressing issue to attend to."

"More pressing than losing your leadership?" The secretary's eyes widened.

"Yes," replied Willow gravely. "But I'll join you as soon as I can."

She ushered Bumble and the still invisible Toby through an inner door and into her office. Bumble looked around with interest; obviously she'd never had the chance to see it before. With burgundy carpets and dark furniture, it was comfortable and elegant without being extravagant. They barely had time to step inside, however, before the walls started closing in on them.

"Intruder alert! Intruder alert!" came a voice.

Within seconds, the three of them were trapped in a room no larger than an armchair. Toby's bubble burst and he found himself squashed between a wall and Bumble; precisely which part of Bumble, he didn't want to consider.

"He's not an intruder! I brought him here." Willow struggled in vain to reach for her wand.

"Earthen in Little Witchery! Earthen in Little Witchery!" said the voice.

"He's here to help us!"

"What is the password?"

"Silver blood."

The walls relented and slid back a couple of feet. Toby took in a deep breath, filling his squashed lungs with air.

"Mercy me," muttered Bumble, her chest heaving.

A shimmering figure appeared before them. It was the double of Witch Willow. "How is the Earthen helping you?" it asked.

"Witch Skylark has been captured. Toby has been kind enough to assist us."

"You don't know you can trust him."

"Really! I did not create you to overrule me. We don't have time for this. Now restore my office to normal!"

The figure regarded Willow coolly.

Bumble gave a yelp. A green vine snaked out of the wall and wrapped itself around her wrist. She tried to pull herself free, but it held tight. More tendrils crept out of the wall and slithered around the witch, writhing and binding her tight. With a high-pitched squeak, Barnaby darted out of Bumble's cloak and fluttered around their heads. Toby backed into a corner, shielding his face.

Willow held her wand aloft:

Free this witch
Stop your fight
Release your grip
And end her fright.

The spell hit a vine. There was a small puff of smoke, and then the vine, uncharred, continued wriggling around Bumble.

Replica Willow gave a low laugh. "You created me! I know your magic inside out. You will never win."

"Let her go!" Willow strode over to Bumble and grasped the green coils. They curled around her own arms, spreading over her body. The Head Witch squirmed and thrashed, but the tendrils continued to bind them.

Keeping low to avoid the flapping bat, Toby

threw himself at Replica Willow, shot through her and careered into the wall. *What the ...?* He stood up rubbing his elbow. She was still standing in exactly the same position. Toby put his finger against her – it went right through, and her image was reflected on his arm. *A hologram!*

Bumble let out another groan. She lay on the floor, a giant green chrysalis. Only her face remained visible, but that, too, would soon be suffocated. Toby hesitated, if he tried to untangle her, he would become as trapped as she was. Bumble's eyes bulged. He did not have time to think. Grabbing Willow's broomstick from the floor, he hit the vines protruding from the wall. Whack whack! At once, they stopped writhing. Whack whack! Toby dropped the broom and tugged at the coils wrapped around the witches. They disintegrated and a rotting smell filled the air. Bits of green fell to the ground and vanished. Within minutes, there was no sign they'd ever existed.

Toby frowned. Why had that been so easy?

"The Earthen has proved he is trustworthy. Intruder alert will be lifted," announced Replica Willow. Then she disappeared.

A test! It had been a test. All that, just to see if he would help the witches.

Noiselessly, the walls slid outwards and the office was restored to normal once more.

"I think I may have set the security measures a little too high," remarked Willow, getting up and smoothing down her dress.

Bumble pulled herself to a sitting position and wiped her glistening, red forehead. "A little?" she spluttered. "You almost killed me."

Barnaby flew at Toby, and the boy threw up his arms in self-defence. The bat landed on his hair, hung upside down and nuzzled his ear. Toby stiffened.

"Look! He's thanking you for saving me," beamed Bumble.

Toby eyed the creature's fangs right next to his cheek. "Um, that's OK."

With a flap of wings, Barnaby retreated into Bumble's cloak. Toby rubbed his scalp where the bat's claws had dug in.

"Now we really must get on," said Willow and pulled a key from around her neck.

CHAPTER EIGHTEEN

Willow walked over to a large cupboard set into the corner of the room. "Toby, I have two magical tools that will help you if you are to rescue Skylark." Inserting the key, she unlocked the ornate wooden door. It opened to reveal another locked door. Holding the tip of her wand against it, she murmured an inaudible chant. The second door swung open with a click.

While Willow rummaged inside the closet, Toby strained to see its contents. Surely a cupboard with two locked doors must contain great secrets? Before he could glimpse anything, the Head Witch extracted two items and pushed the doors closed. Placing one of the objects on her desk, she held the other out in front of her. It was cylindrical and silver, similar to a small telescope, but with blades, like those of a fan, protruding from one end. "This is a secret-seeker."

"Oooh!" Bumble leant forwards to get a better look.

Willow continued. "It enables the user to pass through any locked door without possession of a wand.

Let me demonstrate."

She took a wooden box from her desk, placed it by her feet and waved her wand. Within seconds, the box had grown into a door. Holding one end of the secret-seeker to the vertical surface, Willow turned the blades slowly while chanting:

Through this door
Let me stride
Make me a hole
Tall and wide.

A hole appeared around the secret-seeker and spread outwards until it covered most of the door. Willow stepped through gracefully, and the hole closed behind her.

"Your turn." She handed the object to Toby.

After a pause, he took it and stood in front of the door, shuffling his feet.

"Now, you need to summon all of your energy and use it to will a hole to form."

Toby held the secret-seeker to the door, rotated the blades and, with regular prompts from Willow, mumbled the chant. A small hole materialised in the door and then closed.

Willow sighed. "You didn't try to feel it!"

Toby was tempted to throw the secret-seeker at Willow and refuse to help anymore. But the picture in his pocket rustled, and his fingers closed around it.

Skylark. The beautiful girl who needed rescuing. Who needed *him* to rescue her. If he saved her, he would be her hero. He turned back to the door.

"Now," directed Willow, "you need to imagine you are driving the secret-seeker into the door and forcing an opening to appear."

Toby closed his eyes and tried to concentrate on his body's energy. He visualised it pulsing through his veins, down his arms and through the secret-seeker, rippling in tiny golden waves and opening a hole in the door. A gap formed, not as large as the one Willow had created, yet big enough to squeeze through. He was about to do just that, when Willow grabbed his shoulder.

"Best not," she said. "You should only pass through a hole which is large enough to step through. They don't stay open very long, and if one closed with your arm or leg still the other side of the door … well … the consequences could be rather unpleasant."

Toby gaped. Was Willow suggesting he was at risk of losing a limb?

"I should also mention," continued the Head Witch in a light tone, "that secret-seekers are very difficult to create and thus extremely rare. Each one contains only ten uses and, seeing as we've already utilised three, I suggest you save the rest for the rescue mission."

Toby was speechless. He wasn't going to get another chance to practise?

Ignoring his look of disbelief, Witch Willow walked briskly to her desk and picked up the other object she'd removed from the cupboard: a black solid cuboid, the size of her hand. She flicked a switch on it, and a soft humming filled the air. The two witches' wands flew out of their pockets. Sitting in a plush, padded chair, Bumble cried out and made a grab for hers, but she was too late, and it attached itself to the black box.

"This is a wand-thief," explained Willow. "It draws all wands within a ten metre radius." As she spoke, a third wand shot through the keyhole of the office door and stuck to the box. "Ah, that'll be my secretary's."

Bumble attempted to pull her wand off the device, but it was fixed as securely as if it were welded.

Willow turned off the switch and the wands fell onto her desk with a clatter. "In the wrong hands, a wand-thief could prove extremely dangerous. I am entrusting this to you, Toby, as I believe you may find it of benefit in locating Skylark's wand once you are in the SMI."

Toby reached out, but Willow placed the wand-thief, along with the secret-seeker, in a satchel beneath her cloak. "No need for you to have it yet," she said with a firm smile.

Clearly the witches were still unsure of him, just as he was of them.

The dinner gong sounded, and Bumble stood up.

"We don't have time to eat," said Willow. "We need to get back to Earth."

"Oh, please," replied Bumble. "I'm as empty as a leaky cauldron. I can't think straight."

Toby knew he should get home, check Mum was OK, but he was as hungry as Bumble. It dawned on him, much to his amazement, that this was the first time he'd thought about his mum since they'd arrived in Little Witchery. There had been so many astonishing things to see and take in. He'd never forgotten his situation before; it had always been there at the back of his mind, a black cloud hanging over him.

Bumble's stomach grumbled.

"Very well, but let's be quick," said Willow.

Bumble fetched three plates of steaming nimnucket stew. With a grimace, Toby dipped his spoon into the strange-looking meal. It had the flavour and texture of potato peelings mixed with cauliflower. And it was grey. Tasty food was never grey. After several mouthfuls, he gave up. Willow regarded his half-eaten meal and pursed her lips with disapproval.

As Bumble cleaned the last morsel from her plate, the secretary knocked on the door.

"Not now," called Willow.

"I'm afraid there's a case of the sparking hiccups in The Bobbin."

"Well, can't the Silver Keepers attend?" asked Willow with exasperation.

136

"They're already there, but they've asked for you. Apparently, it's a severe attack."

Willow sighed. "Tell them I'll be right there."

She pulled a chain from under her dress to reveal a warbler, the same as the one Bumble had used to call Little Witchery from Toby's attic. As Willow held her wand to it, a round mirror on her desk lit up. "You'll be able to see what I can see on this." She turned the mirror to face them. "And I, too, will be able to watch you. So do not move from your chairs. Do not pick anything up in my office. Do not go through any doors. Understood?"

"Do you have to go?" said Toby. "I need to get home. Make sure Mum's OK." He left her alone all day when he was at school, but she didn't usually have a strange witch in the house with her. Witch Hazel better not have disturbed her. *Why had he agreed she could stay?*

"I won't be long." Willow attached the warbler to her chest and picked up her broom. "It'll be quicker to use the turret. I'll never get through the dining hall without every witch wanting to ask me something."

She stood in front of twenty pictures on the wall, each the size of a piece of paper, full of abstract grey shapes and lines. Willow pointed her wand at one and deftly moved them around. The pictures slid up, down, left and right. They swivelled and rotated, too fast for Toby to follow. Within less than a minute, they formed an old, crooked door in the wall. Willow pushed it open with a creak.

Toby moved his attention to the mirror; the Head Witch had entered a small round room. By her feet, something was growing from the ground. A plant? Was Willow being attacked again? No, these vines were silver not green, flowing like molten metal. They twisted and turned, intertwining towards the ceiling, forming a rickety spiral staircase. Up and up Willow climbed, her boots tapping on the steps until she reached the top of a tower. Abruptly, her face appeared in the mirror. "I'll be back soon. And don't move!" Then she launched herself through an oval window and into the air.

CHAPTER NINETEEN

As Willow flew, her warbler showed nothing but sky and the occasional other witch on broomstick. Toby's eyes strayed around the room, landing upon a picture on her desk. The girl, with her wild orange curls, must be the Head Witch's daughter. But who were the man and little boy?

"That's Willow's family," remarked Bumble, noticing his gaze.

Toby frowned. "I haven't seen any men in Little Witchery."

"Oh, we don't live with the wizards! Heavens above."

"What! Why not?"

"Well, you don't live with your father either."

"He's dead!" cried Toby. "He was in a car accident when I was two."

Bumble's hand flew to her mouth. "Oh Toby! I'm so sorry."

"He and my mum were happy. We'd all be living together now if he was … well … you know …"

Bumble reached out to pat his arm, but Toby turned away. In the silence, he could feel her staring at the back of his head.

"Do all Earthens have that?" she asked.

"Have what?"

"A white patch of hair. Like you."

"No." Toby grimaced.

"You don't like it?"

He studied his hands.

Bumble leaned forwards. "It's good to be different."

"Being different is horrible. Being different means you get picked on," Toby muttered.

"Being different is great! Who wants to be the same as everyone else?"

Toby looked up at her. She sat there in her bright patchwork dress, a bat peeping out of her pocket and her head held high.

Bumble smiled at him. "Be proud to be you, Toby," she said gently.

He reached out to fiddle with his tuft of hair, to flatten it down, then he stopped. Lowering his arm, Toby lifted his chin and sat a little straighter.

Bumble pointed towards the mirror. "She's arrived!"

Willow stood inside The Bobbin. Wisps of smoke floated around the shop. Here and there lay the charred remains of wool and fabric. In the midst of it all, sat a chubby gurgling baby in an old-fashioned pushchair

140

with large wooden wheels. Behind her, a witch wrung her hands. "I'm so glad you've come, Witch Willow! We can't get her to stop."

The baby gave a loud hiccup and sparks flew out of her mouth. They hit a ball of wool on the counter, setting it alight.

At once, a Silver Keeper standing by the door held out her wand:

Use the fountain
Put out the fire
Bring me water
Till the flames tire.

A stream of water shot out of her wand, dousing the burning wool. Another plume of smoke billowed into the room.

"Can't you do something?" wailed a witch leaning on the counter. "She's destroying my shop."

Willow pointed her wand at a ball of black wool. It lifted from the shelf and began to unravel. Hovering in the air, threads of yarn danced and intertwined. They formed a body which grew two arms with sharp claws. From the top emerged a head with beady eyes. The black monster glided in front of the pushchair and howled, saliva dripping from its fangs.

The baby opened its mouth to scream and a jet of fire blasted across the room. A stack of rainbow coloured wool burst into flames. But Willow and the

Silver Keeper were prepared and water spurted from their wands.

Thick smoke filled the shop and the inhabitants coughed and spluttered. Willow opened the door letting it drift into the town. "Make sure the Bubble Patrol open the flaps immediately. They'll need to measure the air quality for the next few days."

The Silver Keeper saluted. "Yes, ma'am."

"My unicorn tail yarn, not my unicorn tail yarn," sobbed the shop owner. "It took me one month venturing through the Siberian mountains to find that."

"Now now, Witch Wool," soothed Willow. "We'll send out another exploration party to get some more."

The mother rocked the screaming baby.

"A big scare always does the trick with sparking hiccups," said Willow. She gave a wry smile. "We'll have to watch this one. She's going to have some powerful magic when she's older."

With the drama over in The Bobbin, Bumble began to fidget. "I'm going to see if there's any more nimnucket stew," she said, getting to her feet and waving her empty plate.

As she shut the office door, a draft wafted through the room, and the corner cupboard swung open. Willow hadn't closed it properly after removing the secret-seeker and wand-thief! Toby craned his neck but couldn't see inside. Willow had said to stay where they were, yet Bumble had moved, hadn't she? He glanced at the mirror: Willow was busy tidying The Bobbin. He would just take a quick look, that wouldn't do any harm.

The faint outline of several objects was visible inside the dark cupboard. Toby pulled out the nearest one. It was heavy, and he half dropped, half lowered it to the floor. Like the wand-thief, it was a black cuboid. But it was larger and had a slit running across the middle of the top. On the side was a small round button.

Push it! said a voice inside Toby's head. *Don't push it! You'll get into trouble,* said a second voice. The temptation was too great. As if in slow motion, his fingers moved towards the button and pressed it.

The two halves of the top swung open, and a brilliant white light flooded out. Toby shielded his eyes against the glare. Through his fingers, he saw colours and misty images swirling from the box. Then the flaps closed with a bang and the light disappeared. Cautiously, Toby removed his hand from his face. In front of him stood a door. Not a door like the one Willow had created to practise the secret-seeker, nor the door through which she'd left the office. This one was crumbling and covered in ivy.

In the mirror, Willow was still clearing the shop. She wasn't watching him. Toby tugged at the ivy. It was dense and entangled, but he yanked away several handfuls to reveal a sign. Painted in black dripping ink, it read: THE PLACE OF PAST TRUTHS. More ivy hid a large rusty key.

Turn it! said a voice inside his head. *Don't turn it! It could be dangerous*, said the second voice.

He would just peer inside. That couldn't do any harm, right? With a pounding heart, Toby reached for the key. It ground in the keyhole and the door groaned open. Beyond was nothing but foggy blackness. He took one step over the threshold. Still darkness. Then another.

The fog cleared, and Toby stood in a lane, a garden gate by his side. A chill wind rustled his hair, and he shivered, wrapping his arms around his waist. Above, an owl hooted in the night sky. Night? Why was it night? It was lunchtime. There came the faint sound of voices. They grew louder and closer, raucous and hostile. A group of men carrying flaming torches emerged from the shadows, their boots beating the lane.

Toby inched backwards. Whatever this place was, he'd seen enough. He should get out before anything happened. He turned to leave. The door had gone. Blood drained from his head, and he threw out an arm to steady himself. The pack approached, their eyes narrowed and their mouths grim. Toby was trapped.

He dived over a stone wall into a field and braced himself to flee. But the men marched straight past as if they hadn't seen him. They were so close, he could smell their sweat and feel the heat from their burning torches. The leader kicked the garden gate, and it lurched open, attached by only one hinge. He strode up the path and hammered on the door of the thatched cottage. "I know you're in there, Mabell Rackwood!"

The door opened a crack, and an old lady peered out. "She's not here, Master Smith, and you should know better than this."

"Hold your peace, woman." He pushed her roughly aside. "We're not leaving till we've found her."

Seconds later, they dragged a young woman out, thrashing and screaming.

"No!" wailed the old lady. "Noooooo!"

With a spring in their step, the six men set back along the lane, pulling the woman by her hair, her bare toes trailing in the dust.

What were they doing? Someone needed to stop them! But it was six against one. Toby followed at a distance. The commotion brought inhabitants out of every house they passed. Soon, a long procession followed the group: men, women and children wrapped in blankets or sacks against the cold night. *What was this place?*

They left the lane and tramped across a field. The wet grass soaked the bottom of Toby's trousers, and he shivered again. It didn't feel like summer here. He heard the river before he saw it; the wind blowing up small waves which lapped against the bank. The men stopped and the straggling visitors slowed, jostling for position as they neared the water. There was no cover for Toby. No walls or trees or bushes. Nowhere to hide if someone glanced behind. But the people were focused on the action in front, craning their necks, their mouths set in grim lines.

The woman was listless now, moaning faintly as her hands and feet were tied together.

Murmurs rippled through the crowd. "She's a witch, I tell you." A man nudged his wife.

"She's the one spoilt our barley. And she soured your milk, Mistress Godfray."

"She spread the pox through the village, mark my words."

A little boy tugged at his father's sleeve. "What's happening, Daddy?"

The man hoisted him onto his shoulders. "If she floats, then she's a witch. If she sinks, then she's not."

The boy's eyes went as round as the moon overhead.

With a large splash, the woman was thrown into the river. She disappeared from view, and, for a few long moments, the water was calm. The crowd leant forward as one, holding its breath, faces illuminated in the torchlight. Then the woman resurfaced, gasping for air.

The villagers erupted, wild animals baying for blood. "Witch! Witch! Witch!" they chorused. "Hang her! Burn her!"

Toby edged away as the crowd surged and pulsed

with electricity. How could people be so savage? And then a hand grabbed his shoulder from behind.

CHAPTER TWENTY

Toby struggled and shook, trying to wrench himself free but fingernails dug into his flesh. They dragged him backwards, backwards, and through a door. Then he was in bright light, lying on a thick carpet in a warm room.

Toby screwed up his eyes, unable to see after the dark night.

"If you are going to enter a locked door, it is always wise to take the key," boomed Willow's voice. "Better yet, don't enter a locked door without permission, particularly when you have been told not to."

Toby squinted at the Head Witch standing over him, hands on her hips. "I'm sorry," he mumbled. "I was just having a look, I didn't mean to get stuck there."

"When I say don't move, I mean don't move," continued Willow, turning to a red-faced Bumble. "It's for your own good."

"Sorry, Witch Willow." Bumble's shoulders drooped.

"What is that place?" asked Toby.

"The Place of Past Truths is where we store the memories of witches who watched their sisters drown or burn at the stake many centuries ago."

"So, what I saw, that *really* happened?"

"Yes. The memories have been passed down from generation to generation to remind new witches of the danger of Earthens."

Toby wanted to stick up for his fellow human race, to say they weren't all bad, but after what he'd just seen, he had nothing to say.

"Now, we've wasted enough time already. We must get on." Willow placed Toby in an invisible bubble and strode out of the office.

In the middle of the square stood Witch Ebonia. Above her, an emerald banner with the words '*It's Time for Action*' danced in front of the fountain. Then the bold, black letters soaked into the material, blurring and fading. '*Vote Ebonia*' appeared on the banner before this too was absorbed. Then came an image: witches, wands raised, standing victorious over a crowd of Earthens.

Willow gave a sharp intake of breath. Bumble chewed her lip.

"If Ebonia becomes Head Witch," whispered Toby, "are you going to attack us?"

"She won't win. It's as likely as an orange tibtab. But even if she did, not many of the clan wish to enter a war with Earthens. You are safe."

Ebonia opened her hand, and a hundred emerald leaflets flew into the sky. They darted across the town swooping around roofs and diving into letterboxes.

"She's been planning this for months!" wailed Bumble.

Willow set her mouth in a grim line and walked past Ebonia without a word.

Toby's feet ached. Willow was following a different route from earlier, and it was taking ages. They came upon a street where a house stood out from the others. Or rather, it didn't stand out and that's what set it apart. Whereas all the other houses buzzed with flamboyant colours and character, this dwelling was grey and seemed, well, empty of personality. Willow stopped in front of it. Although it was warm and sunny inside Little Witchery, standing outside this house, there was an eerie chill.

Willow cleared her throat. "You may have heard Witch Hazel mention two witches were with Daisy when she went missing?"

Toby nodded before realising she couldn't see him. "Yes," he whispered.

"We believe they, too, might have been captured by the SMI. This house belongs, or should I say belonged, to one of them – Witch Ivy. You have noticed a witch's residence takes on the character of its inhabitant? Well, it is clear to see from this house,

Witch Ivy is no longer alive."

Toby needed no further explanation. It was obvious. The houses around him hummed with the life of their owners. This one was clearly dead. He felt sick. Was Witch Ivy the woman at the SMI window two years ago? Probably. And what had Toby done? Nothing. She had been screaming for help and he'd ignored her. He had been so caught up in his own problems, his mum's illness. And now the witch was dead. *There was nothing you could have done about it. Nobody would have believed you.* But the guilt lay heavy in his stomach.

Witch Willow walked on a few metres before pausing at the next house. It, too, was different; not dead like that of Witch Ivy's residence, yet not buzzing with life either. It emitted the faintest of greens, but no personality shone through.

"This belongs to Witch Ivy's sister, Witch Holly. She is the other witch who went missing," said Willow. "We have reason to believe that Witch Holly is still alive. You can see her house is in a semi-conscious state, biding its time until her hoped for return."

The building did seem to be slumbering, breathing slowly and waiting for the reappearance of its mistress.

"We believe Witch Daisy is still alive too. You may have seen how her room at Witch Wing's house was also sleeping?" Willow continued. "We wonder, we hope, that, if you do enter the SMI, you might find Holly and Daisy there too."

A whirring filled the air. Beneath Toby's feet, the road vibrated, and his teeth rattled in his head.

"Hold onto something!" shouted Willow, clutching a fence post.

Bumble wrapped her arms around a nearby tree trunk. But Toby, standing in the middle of the road had nothing to grasp. He took several stumbling steps, and then the road started to shake violently. Falling to his knees, Toby crawled across the smooth concrete and grabbed part of a wall. He was just in time. The world spun: a blur of houses, trees and fences flashing past him. He clung to the bricks for dear life. A stray marble flew out of his pocket, spiralling away in ever increasing circles. "Look out!"

"Oof! What was that?" Bumble rubbed her cheek.

Just when Toby thought his hair might be ripped from his scalp, the world slowed. With a final whirr, it ground to a halt. Willow let go of the fence post and continued walking with the poise of a ballerina and not someone who had just got off a wild rollercoaster ride. Bumble followed behind, swaying from left to right. In her pocket, Barnaby let out a series of moans. Head spinning, Toby wobbled after them, like a baby giraffe taking its first faltering steps.

"But the roads only shifted a few days ago!" said Bumble once she had got her breath back.

"I suspect the town can detect an Earthen in its

midst," replied Willow.

"What happened?" said Toby.

"Every few weeks, the roads change places," explained the Head Witch. "So that, if we are ever invaded, the intruders would lose their way. Now, I think you have seen enough of Little Witchery. It's time we returned to Earth."

She held out her wand.

The roads have changed
So lead us all
The quickest route
To the entrance hall.

The tip of her wand shone yellow and vibrated. It pulled Willow along the road like a dog straining at the leash. At the corner, the wand turned sharply to the left.

"This way!" she called to Bumble and Toby who were some way behind, still trying to find their feet.

Passing Bumble's house, a bundle of fur shot out to greet them again. Bumble fondled its ears as it wagged its tail with excitement. "Sorry Cuddles. I know it's not fair, but I've got to leave you here again. I'll be back soon, I promise."

The bird-dog put its tail between its legs and whimpered. "Oh Cuddles! I'm sorry!" Bumble put her hand to her mouth.

Toby rolled his eyes. *Cuddles?* What a ridiculous

name for such a magnificent beast. Trust Bumble.

"Wait a moment," said Willow. "I think I might have an idea. Toby, do you fancy a change to broomstick flying on the way home?"

CHAPTER TWENTY-ONE

Flying on a Golden Retrieagle was a hundred times better than balancing on a wooden stick the width of a toothbrush. Cuddles' back was broad and stable, and his wings flapped sturdily either side of Toby. Ahead, Willow and Bumble bobbed on their brooms, two giant ravens … or was it cravens?

As they flew, Toby reflected on all he'd seen in Little Witchery. Had Witch Ivy died at the hands of the SMI while he'd been busy shutting himself down, making sure he thought about nothing, felt nothing? What was it that Roger had said about him on the last day of term? *'You don't care about anything anymore.'* Toby traced a finger in Cuddles' fur. What had happened to him?

Images flooded his mind: him, Roger and Jazz, the three musketeers, cycling through the streets, whooping as if they owned the place. Him and Roger turning their water guns on Jazz as she hid behind the shed, laughing so hard their cheeks ached. And then, Roger and Jazz calling round, inviting him to a barbecue, a game of dodgeball … and him shutting the door in their faces, again and again. He always said he couldn't, he had to look after Mum. But that wasn't always true, was it? Sometimes Toby was free, yet he still didn't go out. It was time to stop hiding from life. The witches needed him. Skylark needed him.

They lost height and the rooftops grew larger below them. Abruptly, Cuddles stopped flying and hovered, staring straight down.

"Um, Bumble! Willow?" called Toby.

The two witches turned. "Quick, Bumble. Stop him!" cried Willow. "He's about to dive."

She was too late. Cuddles dropped from the sky like a stone, hurtling towards the Earth. Toby clung to his back, lying face down and clutching great handfuls of fur. Houses and gardens grew closer and closer.

Well, this is it, thought Toby. I'm going to die. I'm going to crash headfirst into a vegetable patch, my brains splattered over the cabbages.

Toby's leg brushed a potato plant, and then Cuddles had changed direction and was soaring upwards again, a mouse in his jaws. Toby's heart hammered in his mouth. His stomach, however, seemed to have been left on the ground.

"Well, he's never done that before," remarked Bumble as they rejoined the witches in the sky. "I keep him well fed. Still, he is part eagle; hunting is his natural instinct."

Toby couldn't reply. His voice appeared also to have been left behind on Cuddles' sudden nosedive.

Maybe broomstick flying was safer than riding a Golden Retrieagle after all.

Toby toppled into his kitchen and collapsed onto a chair. It took a few moments to get his bearings, and when he did, his jaw dropped. The room had been struck by a great catastrophe. Dirty pots and pans covered every surface. On the hob, a giant saucepan bubbled over. Blue goo splattered both ceiling and floor. Amidst it all, also coated in blue splodges, stood Witch Hazel. "I thought I would prepare us all a little sustenance … only I couldn't quite get the hang of this cooking machine." She looked at the floor, unable to meet their eyes.

Didn't he have enough to deal with? Toby had been completely caught up in all the extraordinary events of Little Witchery. But now the reality of his life hit him once again. It enveloped him like a heavy cloak and everything felt too much. He buried his face in his hands. He didn't want to have to deal with this, have to deal with anything anymore. He let out a strangled gulp.

"It must be difficult for you with your mother ill," said Willow gently.

"It all happened so quickly!" choked Toby. "One day she was fine. And the next she couldn't get to work. Within a week, she was stuck in bed." He'd never spoken to anyone about this before. Now the floodgates were open, his words tumbled out. "The

157

doctor came. Asked questions. Did blood tests. But he couldn't do anything. She *just* has post-viral fatigue, he said. She *just* needs rest and she'll get better."

Another gulp. Toby wiped his nose. "But she hasn't got better! She's so fatigued. And in pain. And now they say it's M.E. So we've been left without help. I can't tell anyone because they might take me away. I don't want to leave my mum! This is my home. I belong here. I belong with her. So it's just the two of us. And I have to do everything."

Bumble rushed forwards, but Willow motioned her back.

The kitchen was quiet. The silence roared at him: *Don't say it! Don't say it!* Toby took a deep breath and grabbed hold of his courage. "It's tough … REALLY tough." His voice was loud and defiant.

There. He'd said it. He'd finally admitted it. To himself. And to someone else. But instead of feeling foolish, a wave of relief swept through Toby. His shoulders gave way, his spine loosened. Like a row of dominoes being knocked down, muscle after muscle from his head to his feet gave a sigh and let go. Had he been tense all these years, clenching every cell of his body?

Witch Hazel placed a hand on his shoulder. "I understand." Then she removed her hand, leaving a blue stain on his top.

Trust the witches – making a mess even when trying to help. Toby could only smile.

158

Willow raised her wand, and at once the kitchen came alive. Four sponges rose from the sink and dashed off in every direction. One set to work scrubbing the walls, another the ceiling. One feisty cloth even attempted to clean up Hazel. Squinting through her spattered spectacles, she tried to dodge its soapy clutches and bat it away. Arms flailing, legs hopping, she looked like she was doing a crazy dance. In five minutes, the kitchen was spotless, much cleaner than it had ever been on Toby's watch. The black work surfaces and white tiled walls gleamed, and his reflection shone back at him everywhere he turned.

"How about some nice sprugel soup then?" asked Hazel as she ladled it into bowls.

"Um, I better not," said Toby. "My mum will wonder why I'm not hungry when I eat with her later." Nimnucket stew was quite enough witch food for him for one day. So, as the witches slurped the blue concoction, he rustled up some pasta for his own dinner.

Toby carried the plates up to his mum's bedroom; she was already sitting up against the pillows. She took her meal but didn't lift her fork. "How was your day?"

"Fine," mumbled Toby. "Cycled round town with Roger, went to the park, you know the kind of thing."

"And why has there been a strange woman in my house?" she asked.

He almost choked on his mouthful of pasta. "W-w-what? There's no one in the house."

159

"Don't lie to me. A little woman with white hair peered into my bedroom this afternoon. *Just wanted to check I was alright'*."

Toby gaped. *Witch Hazel had done what?* "Um, she's a friend's gran. She wanted to help out. Sorry Mum! I told her she didn't need to, but she insisted."

"I see." His mum arched her eyebrow. "And how come this 'friend's gran' does magic?"

Toby's plate wobbled on his knees, spilling tomato sauce on the bedcovers. "She … magic … what …?"

"Did you look at the garden when you got home this evening? Our plant pots have miraculously grown flowers. Don't get me wrong, they're very pretty. I've just never seen flowers grow so quickly before. Come to think of it, I'd never seen someone use a wand before either."

Toby's jaw hit his chest.

"You know about the witches, don't you?" said his mum quietly.

"The who? No! No, I don't know anything."

Mum's eyes pierced right in to him, and Toby squirmed.

"So what have you really been doing today?" she asked.

He bit his lip. "*You* know about the witches?"

"I worked at the SMI, for goodness' sake! Of course I know about witches! But how do *you* know about them?"

"One landed in our attic, Mum. The other day."

"In our attic!" Her fork clattered onto her plate.

"The SMI have captured her niece. That telescope thing," Toby pointed out of the bedroom window, "it shoots them down."

"I know! Witches are dangerous. You need to be careful."

"No they're not! Annoying, maybe. Actually, *really* annoying. But they don't mean any harm."

"How do you know that? You can't trust them!"

"I've spent the last two days with them! They just want to be left alone, to be free. But Earthens, that's humans, keep interfering. We're the dangerous ones!"

His mum frowned as Toby ploughed on. "Do you know what the SMI does to them?"

"Not really. They never captured one when I worked there."

"They experiment on them! And worse. The witches are people, like me and you. How could you have even worked there?"

His mum slumped back, resting her head on the pillows. "We were told ... our work for the SMI ... it was contributing to the nation's security. I did see some things I didn't agree with." She closed her eyes as if the memory pained her. "But I chose to ignore them. I had no skills, no training to get a well-paid post somewhere, and my SMI cleaning job paid much better than any other cleaning work around here ... they pay you to keep quiet, I guess ... I think that's why they still pay me – to keep quiet. I made a choice … so that I could give my son the best upbringing possible."

Toby's stomach churned: Mum had chosen him over the witches … and what was he about to choose?

"So, what's going to happen to the witch the SMI has captured?" she said.

"The witches want to rescue her but …"

"But the witch detector means they can't so they want you to?"

Toby nodded glumly.

His mum rubbed her forehead. "Why you? How did you manage to get yourself into this mess?"

"I keep asking myself the same question," he replied with a wry smile.

"But our income comes from the SMI! They own our house."

"I know," Toby said quietly.

For several minutes, there was only the sound of the clink of their cutlery as they tried to eat their meal. Toby forced some pasta into his mouth. Was he making the wrong decision? How could he do this to Mum, now that she knew?

"When? When are you supposed to rescue her?" his mum burst out.

"Tonight."

"Tonight? So soon!"

"The SMI is about to experiment on Skylark."

"Skylark? That's a pretty name. How old is she?"

"Fifteen. She *is* pretty."

"Is she now?" His mum's lips twitched.

Toby pulled a face and his cheeks grew hot.

"Her little sister went missing near the SMI two years ago. The witches think she might be there too. I met their mum; she was distraught. Can you imagine? Both her children missing."

"How old is her sister?"

"Daisy? She's eight."

Toby's mum put her hand to her mouth. "So young! A whole four years younger than you, and I still see you as my baby."

"I'm not Mum, not anymore."

"I know sweetheart. You've had to grow up far too fast. You're my hero and I'm so grateful for everything you do."

A lump caught in Toby's chest and he turned away.

The witch detector rotated on top of the SMI above the garden hedge. Will I be seeing you soon, Toby? it hissed. Or don't you have the nerve? Let's find out what you're really made of.

"How are you even going to get over No-man's-land?" his mum asked.

"Broomstick."

"Oh, of course. Broomstick. Why ever didn't I think of that?" She winked.

Toby gave a small smile.

"Toby, promise me you'll stay safe. I mean, if

anything happens, if you're about to get into trouble, just please get yourself out of there. OK?"

"So you don't mind then?"

"Mind? I'm petrified. But you've already made the decision, haven't you? And all I can think right now is, how did I manage to bring up such an amazing son?"

"I don't understand. I'm going against what you wanted me to do. I'm risking our income." Toby chewed his lip.

"Sometimes, there is no right answer to a problem. Sometimes, you just have to do what you believe is best. And you've chosen to do something that is best for someone else, not yourself. Be careful and I'll see you on the other side."

Toby sat alone in the garden, on their rickety bench with its missing slats. He needed some time to steel himself for the terrifying nocturnal mission ahead. Was he doing the right thing? And what exactly would happen? He would fly over the hedge, and hopefully get into the building. But then? He would have to play it by ear and hope for the best. As long as he didn't get caught, everything would be OK, wouldn't it?

And if he found the camera Dacker had used, Toby would destroy the video so no one would ever see it. He couldn't protect Mum from the illness, but he could protect her from this. She had lost so much already, she would not lose her son to the authorities as well.

Checking none of the witches were watching, Toby retrieved the picture from his pocket. He stared at Skylark, her golden tresses of hair shining like a halo in the evening sun. So this was the girl he was to rescue. And if he did succeed, think how delighted she would be with him. She would look with adoration and gratitude at him, her saviour. For once, Toby allowed himself to float away on a daydream, allowed it to wrap its enchanting tendrils around him and carry him off to the land of clouds.

CHAPTER TWENTY-TWO

Toby had been watching the clock for hours, his heart thumping in time with the second hand. 10.30pm had finally come and, clothed in black from head to toe, he stood astride Willow's broomstick in his back garden. They'd tried to prepare for all eventualities. If his bubble burst and the SMI had CCTV, only Toby's eyes would be visible through the hole in his balaclava. To avoid detection further, he wore gloves so he'd leave no fingerprints. The secret-seeker and wand-thief were nestled in his trouser pockets.

Steered by Witch Willow, Toby rode down the garden and over the hedge. Now a little more used to broomstick flying, he was able to stay upright but still had to cling on for dear life. He flew over the narrow strip of No-man's-land and the high barbed wire fence before landing on the grass just inside the SMI perimeter. Thank goodness Willow hadn't lost control of the broomstick this time.

Toby looked warily around. It was a clear night and the moon was bright. Lamps scattered around the SMI grounds gave off additional light. There were two vehicles in the car park. Toby's heart sank. There couldn't still be people at work in the building on a Sunday, could there? Resisting the urge to return home there and then, he tiptoed across the grass towards the main door.

Night-time was so quiet! During the day, he didn't notice the everyday sounds that must always be present: the hum of distant traffic, the drone of an overhead plane. But now these sounds were absent, Toby missed them. There was nothing to mask the noises he made. The scrunch of his shoes as he crossed the gravel driveway, amplified in the silence, sounded like thunder.

Reaching the door, Toby bent to put down the broomstick and stopped. He couldn't put it down! It would burst his bubble as it passed through. Why hadn't they thought of this? He would have to take it with him. Carrying a broomstick was *not* going to make it easy to sneak around.

Toby peered through the frosted glass but could see nothing in the darkness beyond. Trembling, he pulled the secret-seeker from his pocket and held it to the door. What had Willow said? '*Summon up all your energy! Force a hole to open!*' There was no room for error. He had to get it right. It didn't help that he was wearing gloves. Toby drew in a deep breath, turned the blades and chanted the words he'd memorised:

Through this door

Let me stride
Make me a hole
Tall and wide.

With his mind, he channelled all his body's energy along the secret-seeker, willing an opening to form. It was surprisingly draining. Toby let out his breath as a large hole materialised in the door. He stepped promptly through, holding the broomstick upright, before the hole closed behind him.

As he entered the building, lights flared up and down the corridor. Toby froze, even though his invisible bubble was still intact. After a few seconds, they went out. He moved and, once again, he was thrown into bright light. *Oh no!* Motion sensitive lamps. Just the thing to draw attention to his presence in the building if anyone was around.

There was nothing for it but to carry on while the fluorescent lamps illuminated the dark. To Toby's left lay a small reception area, closed for the night. A corridor stretched out before him. He crept forwards. The passageway was clean and uncluttered, a smell of antiseptic in the air. Every few metres, on either side, stood a door, each labelled with a name, a title, or a department: '*Stockroom*', '*Office Manager*' … Toby listened at a few of the doors and tried the handles. Everywhere was silent and every latch was locked. He could have used the secret-seeker to enter some of the rooms, but that would have taken far too long and, besides, it had only a limited number of uses.

The lino on the floor had been polished, and Toby's shoes squeaked with every step. Best to carry them and continue in his socks. He slipped and slid along, unsteady on his feet; but at least he made no sound.

Toby proceeded along the corridor glancing from left to right – none of the door labels seemed to be what he was looking for. He came to '*Mr Dackman – Associate Director*'. Dacker's father. Was that where the video camera would be hidden? Probably. Should he go in? Find and destroy the degrading footage of Mum? He knew he should locate Skylark first, but the video could be right under his nose. Toby was reaching for the secret-seeker in his pocket when a small movement ahead made him start in alarm. Somebody was peering around the end of the corridor.

The hairs on Toby's arms stood on end as if they were statically charged. Why was someone in the building at this time of night? The person walked towards him – it was the Director of the SMI. Toby had seen him through the skylight the previous evening. The man was medium height but stocky. His hard eyes roamed the corridor, a suspicious look on his face. What had alerted him? The light of the motion sensitive lamps? Toby shuffled backwards. In his socks and attempting to make no sound, his speed was slow, and the Director gained on him with every step.

The corridor wasn't wide, and if the man came

much closer, he would bump into the invisible Toby and burst his bubble. Toby lifted the broomstick, ready to strike out if needed. His heart thundered in his ears; it was a wonder the Director couldn't hear it. When the man was no further than two metres away, there came a faint shout. "JB?"

The Director stopped. "Yeh?"

"Can you come here a sec?" the voice replied. *Was that Dacker's dad?*

The Director gave the corridor one more searching look and then retreated. He didn't turn his back and kept his eyes in front until he'd vanished from sight around the corner.

Slipping and sliding in his socks, Toby hurried towards the main entrance. There was no way he could continue with people in the building, he would have to return later or another evening. He was pulling the secret-seeker from his pocket when he stopped. If his calculations were correct, it contained six more usages. If he were to leave now and come back later, that would use two. Then he would need another for the final exit ... which left him with three. That would let him enter at the most one or two rooms in the search for Skylark and the video. *Not enough!*

Toby turned around once again and reshuffled along the hall. He would go to the end and see what was around the corner before choosing whether to carry on. If there was the slightest chance he might be discovered, then he would leave. He was not going to

170

risk getting himself, and Mum, into trouble.

He continued to glance at each door he passed, but none of them seemed right. At the room labelled 'Research Department', Toby paused – would they be keeping Skylark there? He would investigate further, should he find nothing else. The deeper he ventured, the more sinister the names on the doors became. 'Waste Disposal', 'Sterilisation Unit', 'Experimentation Laboratory'. What did they mean? What was the SMI doing to witches?

As Toby drew closer to the end of the corridor, the sound of voices floated towards him again.

"I thought I heard something and the lights came on. Couldn't see anything though." That was the Director.

"Well, why don't you hit the security button? Just in case." That must be Dacker's dad.

There came a beep, beep, beep and then a faint whirring behind Toby. He shot round and his mouth dropped open. There was a gaping hole in the ground by the front door. The corridor floor was sliding away! And fast. It was withdrawing into itself, and the hole was getting nearer and nearer to Toby. Soon there would only be walls and nowhere to stand at all.

Toby ran. But his socks were too slippery and he lost his balance, his arms circling like windmill sails. As he was about to hit the floor, the strangest thing happened: his bubble bounced. Over and over rolled the bubble, and over and over went Toby, head over heels, a giant hamster in a runaway exercise ball. Behind him, the floor continued to slide away, the hole gaining on him quicker than he was rolling.

Where the corridor turned to the right, Toby in his ball shot straight on. He hit the wall and rebounded off it. By now, the floor had completely disappeared. A mess of sprawling limbs and broomstick, he fell into the black abyss.

CHAPTER TWENTY-THREE

Toby spun downwards with no idea which way was up, his brain as jumbled as the rest of him. He hit the ground with a small bounce, the bubble cushioning his fall and then it burst with a loud pop.

He lay winded in the dark, staring upwards. High above, the corridor lights blurred and danced on his retinas. Beneath, the floor was cold and rough. Toby pushed himself to a sitting position, gulping in deep breaths. *What the heck just happened?* He'd hardly got into the building and now he was in a worse mess than when he'd started. He rubbed his aching back. At least he hadn't broken anything. It was a good job Willow had made such a strong bubble.

Where was he? The corridor lamps filtered down through the hole, lighting up a small space around him. There was nothing but the gravelly surface on which he sat. Beyond that was utter darkness. *Why hadn't he brought a torch!* Toby heaved himself to his feet and pulled out his mobile phone. Taking a deep breath, he set off to search the gloom.

Every few steps, he pointed the screen light to the

left, right, above and below. It was so feeble, he couldn't see further than a couple of metres. Toby's pulse raced, terrified at what might be just out of sight ready to pounce, But the place was empty. And it was vast. He explored so far, the small patch of light from the corridor became a dot in the distance.

After several minutes, he reached a stone wall. Soil crumbled through the cracks. The air smelt of earth and damp. He seemed to be in a basement that spread the entire length of the SMI. Toby followed the wall, trailing his hand along the stone for direction. An object loomed out of the dark in front. His heart leapt into his mouth, but the object didn't move. He crept closer, shining his phone over it. *A chair*. He'd almost had a heart attack over a chair. Toby glanced back at the distant dot of light. Could he climb out into the corridor? Was the chair high enough? He snatched it up and began to run.

The patch of light grew bigger and brighter. Toby was only a few metres away when there came a whirring sound: the floor was sliding over the hole. *No! NO.* Before Toby could reach it, there was a click and the basement ceiling closed above him. Now there was no way out. He was as trapped as Skylark.

Total blackness surrounded him. He couldn't even see his hand in front of his face. There was no sound but the panting of his breath. Fear and anger pulsed inside Toby. He threw the chair onto the ground with a clatter. Then he took a hefty kick at it. In the dark, he missed and sprawled onto the floor by its side.

What was he going to do? Did anyone know he was here? Unlikely. Surely they would have come to put him in handcuffs by now? It didn't look like anyone ever came down here. He was going to die of thirst or starvation or maybe lack of oxygen. With the hole closed, the air was stale and heavy. By the time he was found, he would be a rotting corpse nibbled by rats. *Oh no, please don't let there be rats.* And what would happen to Mum without him to care for her? She would wither away too.

Toby's thoughts went to Roger. *He* wouldn't give up so easily. They'd got out of plenty escapades in the past, even if none of them were quite as life-threatening as this. *Pull yourself together, Tobe.* That's what Roger would say.

Toby sat up. There was still some of the basement to investigate. Maybe there was another exit. He fumbled around on the floor and found the broomstick. He would need it if he were ever able to get out of here. Pulling himself to his feet, Toby flicked on his mobile light once more and headed into the unknown. He shuffled through the empty expanse, his feet thudding on the stone floor. Had he already been this way? Without the light from the corridor, it was impossible to tell. He could even be going round in circles. *Keep going. You can do this. It's only darkness.*

After a couple of minutes, Toby stumbled into a wall. The same wall? Another one? He followed it. A dark shape emerged before him. It was a grey cube with a dirty glass door on the front, like the log burning stove in Roger's living room, only bigger, like a furnace. Toby snorted. They were in the middle of a heatwave. He was wrapped from head to toe in clothing. This was the last thing he needed right now.

He moved on, then stopped and retraced his footsteps, shining his phone light over the stove. A chute led off it into the ceiling. A chimney? Would he fit in it? *Don't be stupid. There's no way you can climb that. And who knows where it leads to.*

Toby pushed the negative thoughts out of his mind. This was his only way out. It was this or nothing. Taking a big breath, he opened the door and stepped inside. If someone lit the furnace right now, he would be roasted to a crisp. But you could only operate it if you were next to it … right? Something crunched under his trainer, and he picked it up: a whitish object with a knobble at one end. Was that … bone? Toby dropped it instantly, the taste of vomit filling his mouth. *What had the SMI burnt in here?* He needed to find Skylark. He pulled himself into the chimney and began to climb.

The chute was smooth, and Toby had to jam his shoes against the ridges between each panel. With his legs bent, his feet in front and his hands behind, he clambered slowly upwards, the broomstick clutched between his knees. It was painstaking work. Sweat poured down his face under his balaclava. Twice, he slipped, sliding down several feet before managing to screech to a halt.

After climbing for several minutes, his foot pressed against a loose panel. Toby gave it a kick and it fell away. He peered out. He was halfway up the wall of a small room. Light seeped under the door. *Should he get out here?* If he carried on in the chimney, he would end up on the roof, on the outside. Then how would he rescue Skylark?

Hauling himself through the gap, Toby jumped down into the room. The glow from his mobile screen lit up two cabinets, bearing the stickers '*Witch Anatomy*' and '*Witch Physiology*'. He pulled open the top drawer of the first and rifled through the contents. It was full of pages and pages of drawings and diagrams. Toby held one in front of his phone light, and his hand flew to his mouth. It was a skeleton. His thoughts went to the white object he'd crunched underfoot in the furnace. *Animal bone? Human bone?* His eyes flicked to the stickers on the cabinet once more. *Witch bone?*

Toby slammed the drawer shut and headed for the door. It was open! Great, he wouldn't have to drain the secret-seeker. He stepped into the corridor and looked both ways. Empty. His shoes were covered in soot, and he took them off. Leaving footprints would be disastrous. Voices drifted towards him. They were coming this way. And Toby was no longer invisible. He turned to dive back into the room.

177

"I just need to lock the Anatomy door." Dacker's dad again.

Toby paused with his glove on the handle, the words '*Anatomy Room*' on the door in front of him. *Nooo!* Dacker's dad was coming to the very room Toby had just been in. He couldn't hide in there.

Opposite stood a staircase and he threw himself towards it. The stairs were as slippery as the floor but, hanging onto the handrail, Toby hauled himself upwards. He stood at the top breathing heavily. The voices were getting louder. Heavy footsteps sounded on the stairs behind him. Ahead of Toby lay another hallway as empty as the one downstairs, with the occasional door on either side. In desperation, he tried the first handle. Locked. He didn't have time to use the secret-seeker. The next door was locked too. And the next. Surely one must be open. The handle of the fourth moved. He lunged inside, shutting the door softly.

"Who are *you*?" came a curious, if haughty voice. Toby spun round. And there she was: the girl he'd come to rescue, looking ghostly in the moonlight that trickled through the skylight. The room was separated in two by iron bars which stretched from floor to ceiling. Skylark sat in a corner, a scared but defiant expression on her face. In her arms, huddled a young girl with hair as blonde as her sister's: Daisy.

Toby's heart beat frantically and not only because of the approaching voices. He was standing in front of the girl of his dreams. Wrapped completely in black clothing, he must appear ridiculous. And he was sweltering, in spite of the building's air conditioning. Beads of perspiration formed on his head and between his fingers, and he had the urge to wrench off his balaclava and gloves. Instead, he pulled the woolly material away from his mouth. "The witches …" He sounded high-pitched and childish. He gritted his teeth and tried again. "The witches sent me to rescue you."

Skylark shot him a look of disdain. Toby frowned; this was not going how he had imagined it. Before he could say anything, the conversation started again right outside the room.

"They'll probably come in here," said Skylark coolly.

Toby scanned the room. It was empty apart from a metal trolley. Hiding the broomstick behind the door, he hurried to the trolley and pulled apart the curtain hanging down the sides. There was nothing but a metal shelf at the bottom. Toby squeezed in. It was a tight fit and the trolley rattled on its wheels. Just in time, he closed the curtain. The door opened and footsteps entered the room.

"Is everything ready for tomorrow then?" It was the Director.

"I need to take this trolley, then everything is prepared," replied Dacker's dad.

Toby's breath quickened. The trolley? The one he was in? He was rolled out of the room and into the corridor.

"I'll be off then," said the Director. "I'll leave you to set the alarm shall I?"

"Yeah, I've got a couple of things to finish off in my office, so I'll be another twenty minutes or so."

"See you tomorrow. Bright and early for the big day!"

"Yep, see you tomorrow."

As the trolley was wheeled down the corridor, Toby clung to its sides, petrified that one of his feet or an elbow would protrude through the curtain. After a few metres, the trolley turned to the right and passed through another doorway. Then the door was closed and locked, leaving Toby alone.

CHAPTER TWENTY-FOUR

Once the sound of footsteps had disappeared up the corridor, Toby crawled from the trolley and stretched out his cramped legs. He would have loved to stay where he was until both men had left the building. But he could not still be inside the SMI once the burglar alarm had been set. He had twenty minutes before Dacker's dad closed up for the night. Twenty minutes to rescue Skylark.

With no skylight, the room was in utter darkness. Toby couldn't even see his own hand held in front of his face. He turned on his phone and squinted around in its feeble light. White tiles covered every wall of the room. In the centre stood a steel bed with a large overhead light. What *was* this place? A small table next to the bed held an array of metal implements. Was he in an operating theatre? What fate awaited Skylark here tomorrow? Toby dug his nails into his palm. He had to help her escape tonight.

Using the secret-seeker, he stepped through the door and into the empty corridor, once again triggering motion sensitive lights. He tiptoed down the hallway.

Which door was it? He hadn't travelled very far. Aha! Here it was, the door which bore no label. This time, it was locked, so out came the secret-seeker once again. Toby had got the hang of it and felt quite a pro at creating a large hole now.

"Is that a secret-seeker?" asked Skylark, her eyes wide, as he stepped into the room. She rose to her feet, eager to see. She was taller than him, standing behind the partition in her light blue dress and black robe. "I've never come across one before! So the witches *did* send you."

A look of admiration filled her face.

This was more like it.

Daisy, however, stayed huddled in the corner, her arms wrapped around her legs, her head drooped.

The bars which imprisoned the witches were solid and secured to both floor and ceiling. Toby held the secret-seeker against them.

"Don't be stupid! You don't expect it to work on curved surfaces, do you?" Skylark shot him a withering look; any regard for him already evaporated.

"Do you want me to help or not? Because I'd be more than happy to get myself out of here without you."

Skylark scowled.

Daisy tiptoed forward. "Please help us," she whispered. "I miss my mum so much."

There was a keyhole at one end of the bars. Toby indicated it, trying to remain patient. "Do you know where the key is?"

Skylark shrugged. "It always hangs on the Director's belt."

"But he's gone!" cried Toby in exasperation.

He peered around the gloomy, moonlit room once more. There was no visible escape route. There were a skylight and a window on his side of the partition, but this was the first floor – too high to jump. Looking out, he realised the room was directly opposite the back of his house. Of course! This must be the window he could see from Mum's bedroom. The window at which he'd seen Skylark … and the other woman ... Witch Ivy he guessed. She wasn't here now though. What had happened to her? Had Willow been right? Did Witch Ivy's house indicate that she was no longer alive?

"Are Witch Ivy and Witch Holly here?" Toby asked.

Daisy shook her head. "We were all captured, but I haven't seen them in a long time." Her hands tightened around the cage bars, her knuckles turning white.

Toby rubbed his eyes, feeling weary. He had come so far and now it seemed there was no hope of saving the sisters.

"If I had my wand …" Skylark trailed off.

"Well, do you know where it is?" Why hadn't she mentioned this before?

"The Director took if off me at the start."

"But he's gone home!" Toby wanted to shout

again, but a memory floated into his head – the Director sitting at his desk, twiddling a stick between his fingers. Was it only last night Toby had seen that, through the skylight from the rooftop? It felt like such a long time ago, so much had happened since then. "I think I might know where it is." Toby turned to leave.

"Promise you'll come back!" Daisy burst out.

"I'll try."

"Promise?" Her blue eyes were large and pleading.

"I promise. I'll be back as quick as I can; we have to get you out before the burglar alarm is set!"

Toby trotted down the stairs. Where was the Director's office? Toby had landed above the main entrance last night, so the office must be near there. He crept along the corridor, even more fearful of bumping into somebody now he was no longer invisible. But he found the Director's door without incident. Toby knocked, just in case. As expected, there came no reply. Again he withdrew the secret-seeker from his pocket. It was rapidly running out.

He passed through the door and stepped into a large room. Tall shelves lined the walls, and, in the centre, sumptuous leather armchairs sat in front of a majestic mahogany desk. Toby walked towards it, the carpet thick and luxurious under his socks. The top of the desk was bare apart from a thick book entitled *How to be Powerful and Successful*. There were no framed family photos, and any paperwork had been tidied away for the night.

A beam of moon through the skylight illuminated a silver pen engraved with the initials '*JB*'. Was it this which he'd seen the Director holding and not a wand at all? A wave of worry swept through Toby. He tried to look in the desk drawers, but they were locked. As he pondered how to open them, he plunged his hands into his pockets. His left hand hit a solid metal object. Toby pulled it out, rubbing his bruised knuckles. *Of course!* The wand-thief! How could he have forgotten it?

Holding the item aloft in the centre of the room, Toby switched it on. A faint humming filled the air. He watched the drawers; if Skylark's wand was in one of them, was the wand-thief powerful enough to overcome the locked latch?

A sound from behind made Toby whirl round. Had someone entered the room? However, the noise was coming from one of the top shelves where a small casket rocked and rattled as if it contained a dangerous animal desperate to escape. It twitched and jumped until the lid sprang open. Out flew a wand, glimmering as it shot across the room, and attached itself to the wand-thief. Toby punched the air in delight.

And then, to his astonishment, another two wands whizzed out of the casket and stuck firmly to the wand-thief. Toby stared at them. Then it dawned on him. Did these wands belong to Witch Holly and Witch Ivy? What had happened to them after Daisy last saw them?

Toby thought of the two houses in Little Witchery, one sleeping and waiting, the other … dead? An icy hand clawed at his insides. He shuddered; time was pressing, he had to get back.

CHAPTER TWENTY-FIVE

Standing outside the door to the witches' prison, Toby hesitated. With a tight chest, he counted how many times he'd used the secret-seeker and his worst fears were confirmed: it had one usage left. Once he'd entered the room, the secret-seeker would become useless. And if none of the three wands concealed up his sleeve belonged to Skylark, then he would be as trapped as she was. No escape from the room, no way to track down the video. *Please let one of the wands be Skylark's*. Then once they were free, she would help him get the video, wouldn't she? Toby took a deep breath and, channelling his energy through the secret-seeker for the final time, passed through the door.

At his return, Skylark, who had been pacing the cage in an agitated manner, paused and watched him expectantly. Removing the three wands from his sleeve, he held them through the bars. With a crow of delight, the witch pounced on one of them. As wand touched owner, a buzz of energy ran up Toby's arm, just like when he'd handed Bumble *her* wand. It reminded him of the power of the witches. Indeed, this witch, who had already been remote and arrogant, seemed to become a dangerous being. She stood tall and proud, a look of defiance and outrage on her face.

Toby held out the remaining two wands to Daisy. "Is one of these yours?"

Skylark rolled her eyes. "She was six when she was captured! Witchettes don't make a wand till they're ten."

"Just think, in two years, I get a wand!" Daisy's face brightened for the first time since Toby had arrived. Then she clutched her sister's cloak, her voice quavering. "I never thought it would happen."

Holding out her wand, Skylark chanted:

Turn this latch
Without key
Unlock the door
And set us free.

The gate in the bars clicked open. Skylark grasped Daisy's hand and strode through. Without acknowledging Toby, the mere mortal who had rescued her, she focused her attention on the door into the corridor.

"Shouldn't you make us invisible?" Toby interrupted.

The witch gave him a glassy stare before placing bubbles around them. With more chanting and another flick of her wand, the door opened and Skylark marched into the corridor. At once there came a beep, beep, beep, and then a deafening alarm wailed into life. They had taken too long! The burglar alarm had been set! Now the whole neighbourhood would know someone was in the building. Skylark faltered and, for the first time, looked to Toby for assistance.

"This way!" he yelled above the din. He grabbed the broomstick, pulled on his shoes and raced for the stairs. Their feet pounded on the steps as they dashed down. They'd travelled only a few metres along the corridor when a metal grille shot out of the ceiling and crashed down to the floor, blocking their escape route. Turning around, a similar grille now barred the way behind too. They were trapped. Toby's shoulders tightened, but he swallowed down his fear. Daisy, who had thought she was going to be free at last, let out a wail and sank to the floor.

"Hush, we'll be eating tibtabs in no time, you'll see." Skylark stroked her sister's head. Wand in hand, she chanted:

> *Turn this latch*
> *Without key*
> *Unlock the door*
> *And set us free.*

Nothing happened. Skylark's eyes widened in surprise that something dare disobey her. She tried again. Still the grille did not move. Now Toby panicked. He shook the gate, to no avail, and then thumped the side wall again and again in anger, bursting his bubble and bruising his fists. *They'd got so far and now there was no escaping.* He would be caught. He and Mum would lose their money, their house.

As Skylark watched him, the gleam of an idea flickered onto her face. "Stand back!" Grabbing Toby's sleeve, she pulled him into the middle of the corridor. She replaced his invisible bubble, then stood in front of the wall and raised her wand.

The bricks trembled and the ground shuddered beneath Toby's feet. The blast of an explosion, loud in the narrow space, sent the three of them floundering backwards, ears ringing. They coughed and spluttered as a suffocating cloud of dust swirled around them. Debris dropped by their feet, and the air cleared to reveal a hole in the wall. Skylark stepped through, Daisy at her side, but Toby stayed put, looking through the metal grille.

"There's something I need to get!" He pointed down the corridor in the direction of Dacker's dad's office where the video camera must be.

Skylark raised her eyebrows. "And how do you propose doing that?" She disappeared through the hole.

A wooden cupboard lined the wall by Toby's side and he gave it an almighty kick, venting his frustration.

It wobbled and the doors flew open, the contents spilling onto the floor. Piles and piles of empty notebooks spread out before Toby. And what was that, the black object? The black object that looked like a ... It couldn't be? Surely not. Toby picked it up. The words 'Darren Dackman' were scrawled on the top. He'd found it! He had the awful humiliating video of his mum in his hands. No one else would ever get to see it. He and Mum were safe.

Toby held the camera to his chest and gave a sigh of relief. Then he remembered. He was still in the SMI. Hanging the camera around his neck, he scrambled over the pile of crumbled bricks and followed the witches into the darkness.

Shine me a beam
Let there be light
In this darkness
Give me sight.

A small ray of light filtered from Skylark's wand to reveal a room filled with tall, white cupboards. Daisy leant against the nearest one, trying to steady her trembling body. The door swung open, and a welcome draught of cool air drifted out. Row upon row of jars lined its shelves. They were in a roomful of fridges.

Toby and Skylark peered inside and read the labels on the jars: 'Witch 001, Witch 001, Witch 001 ... Witch 002, Witch 002, Witch 002 ...' They looked at each other with a frown. Toby picked up one of the jars. Inside, a silver strand in a dark red liquid shimmered in the beam from the wand. Skylark opened the next cupboard: a freezer laden with boxes, also marked 'Witch 001'. Toby's worst suspicions were confirmed. He pushed Daisy back so she couldn't see the contents.

"Come on! We have to get you both out of here!" Toby slammed the door shut and they fled across the room, between the rows of fridges, to the far wall.

Another blast, another cloud of dust. And when it dispersed, a blissful sight: a large hole in the wall and, beyond, freedom! They clambered through and stood for several moments, filling their lungs with the sweet, sweet air of a summer's night. But still the alarm wailed into the night arousing the neighbourhood, still they were not safe. They had to escape the SMI grounds.

Toby and Skylark started to run full pelt along the side of the building, yet Daisy did not follow. She stood rooted to the spot, her breath quick and shallow. After two years in her prison, all she could do was stare with large fearful eyes at the outside world.

Skylark ran back and picked her up. "We're almost free! Think of the tibtabs! And one day you'll get your very own wand." Then Skylark raced after Toby, her sister held tightly in her arms.

By the main door, Toby darted out across the grass, heading for the edge of the enclosure. Now where was his house? From this side, he could see only the perimeter fence and the tall thick hedge beyond. They stretched the entire length of the grounds, and it was impossible to work out where his garden lay.

There was a cry behind him, barely audible above the blare of the alarm. Toby spun round to see a small black object hurtle towards Skylark and miss her head by inches. *The witch detector!* How on earth would the witches be able to escape from the SMI grounds with that on the lookout?

Scowling, Skylark retreated to the cover of the building. Gently, she lowered Daisy to the ground and then ran back out onto the grass. Before the witch detector had time to shoot, Skylark flicked her wand, and the giant contraption erupted in smithereens.

Well that was one way to solve that.

"We need to get out of here!" Toby hissed.

Skylark wasn't listening. She faced the building, wand raised. With a crash, part of the roof collapsed. A flick of the wand, another and another, and the building crumbled.

What was she doing! Toby's stomach writhed in panic, as if there was a snake inside. He and Mum needed the SMI! It provided their income. Their source of life. "No! NO!" Throwing the broomstick to one side, Toby ran towards the witch and grabbed her arm.

Shaking him off, she whipped round. She towered above him, her eyes glinting dangerously, her wand held high. Toby dropped back.

Once again Skylark turned her attentions to the building. She stood there, a majestic queen, her long black cloak flowing from her raised arms and her golden hair lit up in the moonbeam like a crown. Toby could do nothing but watch, fists clenched, as she continued to destroy the SMI. Over and over, Skylark flicked her wand. It was as if she was possessed, riding on a wave of power, fury and delight. As the building collapsed in front of Toby, it was as though his and Mum's life was crumbling around him.

A flash of orange flickered amongst the fallen bricks. The first flames licked the ruins. With each breath of oxygen, the fire grew hungrier and stronger until a ferocious beast raged before them. The burglar alarm cut out, and an eerie quiet took hold, broken only by the hiss and crackle of burning. Smoke billowed towards the three onlookers, and heat scorched their skin, driving them backwards.

A trace of fear crossed Skylark's face as if she'd just realised the enormity of her actions.

"Can't you put it out?" choked Toby.

The whole neighbourhood was going to burn down.

"I don't know how," she whispered. The blood drained from her cheeks and her shoulders hunched. She was now just a child, in need of someone to save her.

"We have to leave!" cried Toby. "I dropped the broomstick. We need to find it."

The three of them stumbled along the perimeter fence peering through the smoke, their eyes stinging. As Toby bent down, scouring the ground, Dacker's video camera bumped against his chest. He hesitated for a moment, then yanked it from around his neck. His throwing was good, but was it good enough? With all his might, he hurled the camera into the heart of the flames. They devoured it in a cloud of sparks. Toby smiled with the sweet sense of revenge. *Four to Toby.*

CHAPTER TWENTY-SIX

Several metres away from where Toby expected, he found the broom. "Here!"

He was about to pick it up, when a male voice shouted right behind them. "Don't move!"

Skylark pulled her wand from her pocket, but the security guard anticipated it. He knocked her hand, sending the wand flying through the air.

"I said, don't move!" he boomed. "Unless you want to be Rocky's next meal."

A giant Alsatian strained at the metal chain in his fist and growled.

Daisy let out a whimper, and Skylark wrapped her arm around her.

"Well you three have been busy." The man nodded at the fire. "Made quite a mess, haven't you?"

In the distance, a siren sounded.

"And there's the fire engine and police, not a moment too soon."

Toby's heart gave a loud thump. *No! No, no.* This was worse than he could have ever imagined. He wasn't just going to get into trouble for breaking into

196

the SMI; the whole place was ablaze, he would be locked up for life. Then who would look after Mum?

The security guard strode towards him. "And who's this fellow, hey? Let's see what you're hiding behind that disguise."

As the man seized the top of the balaclava, Toby grabbed the bottom. He could not let the guy see him! They tussled and fought, grunting and coughing in the thickening smoke. Toby's elbow caught his opponent on the chin, and the man let out a bellow but didn't let go. With a volley of barks, the Alsatian's jaws snapped around Toby's leg, missing his flesh but gripping his trousers. The dog pulled and shook the material like it was a dead rabbit. Toby wobbled, and the security guard, sensing his chance, gave an almighty yank to the balaclava. It slipped upwards revealing Toby's neck, then his chin ...

Out of nowhere, something small and black hurtled out of the night, striking the man on the cheek. He staggered backwards, clutching his face, blood dripping through his fingers. With beating wings and slashing claws, Bumble's bat attacked again and again. The man fell to his knees, covering his head.

The wailing of sirens grew louder. It wouldn't be long before they arrived.

"Let's get out of here!" yelled Toby. But as he reached for the broom, the man let go of Rocky's lead. The snarling Alsatian threw himself at Toby, knocking him flat on his back. They tumbled to the floor, the dog pinning the boy to the ground. Just before the jaws clamped shut on his nose, Toby grabbed Rocky's shoulders. Saliva dripped onto his face as he tried desperately to keep the gnashing teeth at bay. The smell of rotten meat on the dog's breath cut through the smoky air.

Rocky was too strong, and Toby's arms weakened. He couldn't hold him off any longer, and the dog went for the kill. But, just millimetres away, the Alsatian stopped and sniffed. Then he pawed at Toby's pocket.

The Morph Munchies! Witch Wing had insisted he brought one each for Skylark and Daisy. Toby delved into his jumper pocket, Rocky's claws scraping deep wounds in his hand, and pulled out the two biscuits. He threw them as far as he could, and the dog bounded after them.

Trembling, Toby got to his feet. *Where were the witches?* They had been here seconds ago. They appeared through the smog, running towards him.

"My wand!" called Skylark. "I had to find it. Can't fly a broomstick without a wand." She looked around. "Where's the beast gone?"

"Morph Munchies," said Toby. "I gave him some Morph Munchies."

"You did what?" gasped Daisy. "How many?"

"Just two."

The witches inhaled sharply. "You can't give animals Morph Munchies!" cried Skylark. "And you can never eat two at once. Who knows what will happen."

Toby shoved the broom at her. "Let's go!"

They clambered aboard with Toby at the back, and rose into the air, before thudding to the ground again.

"There's too many of us! We're too heavy," said Skylark.

The sirens blared again, they were so close now. And then the gates opened, and a car raced up the drive. But it wasn't a police car. A man sprang from the driver's seat. It was the Director.

"What have you done, you brats!" he shouted, tearing his hair as he gaped at the fire.

He lunged towards the broom.

Skylark brandished her wand. "Keep away!"

The Director backed off, hatred in his eyes. "I knew you were dangerous!" He pointed a finger at Skylark. "But who are you," he spat at Toby, "and why are you helping them?"

"You experiment on them!" Toby replied in a hoarse voice, struggling to breathe through his balaclava in the thick air.

"We have to! You can't trust witches and their magic. Look at what they've done to my building."

"Only because *you* captured them!"

A creature lumbered out of the gloom, his hair standing on end and his body shaking. *Rocky?* Red scaly wings erupted from the dog's back. His snout grew longer and longer, rimmed with dozens of sharp fangs.

"What is that?" screamed the Director. He sprang towards his car. "Don't think you're going to get away with this!"

Toby gripped Skylark's arms. "Fly!"

Clumsily, the broom climbed again, Skylark urging it upwards. Rocky beat his powerful wings, sending gusts of scorching air over the three passengers, and soared into the sky. The broom careered down the inside of the SMI fence, unable to get more than a metre off the ground. The scarlet dragon, mouth wide open, followed in hot pursuit.

"Faster!" cried Toby. He squinted behind through streaming smoke-filled eyes. "He's gaining on us!"

They rocketed around the grounds. Passing the Director's car, Rocky whipped his scaly tail. It crushed the top of the car into a heap of mangled metal.

As they zoomed past the security guard crouched on the ground, Barnaby set his sights on his next victim. Screeching, he raced at the dragon and dug his claws into the snout. With one swipe of the head, Rocky knocked the bat flying. Barnaby plummeted lifeless to the floor.

The dragon let out an almighty roar and sped after the broomstick. With every second, the gap between them narrowed. Toby risked another look behind. The dragon was advancing, nearer and nearer he came until his black beady eyes were staring straight into Toby's blue ones.

Toby's heart hammered. What could he do? *Think. Think.*

The dragon's forked tongue flickered.

Toby took hold of Skylark's cloak. Would his idea work? If he didn't get it right, if he were a millisecond too early or too late, he would be mincemeat.

With a final beat of his wings, Rocky lunged at the broom.

NOW! Toby wrenched the cloak from Skylark's back and threw it over Rocky's head. Blinded, the magnificent monster flailed and flapped, unable to free itself. Then he crashed to Earth, snapping a wing beneath him. A hair-raising howl filled the night sky.

"My garden!" cried Toby. Sweat poured down his cheeks inside the balaclava. "We need to get to my garden. Can the broomstick get over the fence?"

The broom rose, then fell, then rose, then fell again.

"We're too heavy!" wailed Skylark.

A blue light flashed around the neighbourhood as a fire engine pulled into Fir Tree Close with a scream of brakes.

"Try!" yelled Toby. "Try!"

Skylark took in a deep breath, coaxing the broom upwards. As if wading through treacle, they gained height.

Come on. Come on.

With nothing to spare, they cleared the fence. But then something grabbed Toby's dangling trouser leg. Heart in his mouth, he looked down: his trousers had snagged on the barbed wire. He kicked out, trying to wrench himself free. The broomstick jerked and flung Toby into the air. As he fell, his fingers found the end of the stick. He hung from the back, his nails scraping on the wood. The broom dipped and jerked again. Toby lost his grasp and plummeted towards the ground. As he hit the floor, a sharp pain seared through his ankle, and he shouted out in agony.

CHAPTER TWENTY-SEVEN

For several moments, Toby lay there, consumed by the excruciating throbbing in his lower leg. Then the familiar whirr of the SMI gates filtered through his half-dazed state. He forced his mind away from the unbearable pain; where was he? Toby's insides contracted. He'd fallen into No-man's-land – the space between the SMI boundary and the hedge.

A few metres away, on the other side of the fence, Rocky, still wrestling with the cloak, was turning back into a dog. And what was that small black object lying on the grass just out of reach? Its webbed wings were motionless and its fur matted with blood. *Barnaby.* The bat had given his own life for theirs. A lump stuck in Toby's throat. How was he going to tell Bumble?

The gates opened, and in drove a multitude of police cars and fire engines, their flashing lights adding a blue tint to the orange and yellow sparks. Vehicle doors slammed shut and people surged around them. Some grabbed hosepipes while others spread out, their torchlights bobbing, searching for … the culprit? Him? Toby's heart beat faster, and his mind began to race. His bubble had burst long ago. He flattened himself to the ground. It would not be long before he was found.

The Director's car door was wrenched open and he staggered out. "There's three of them. A boy and two witc … girls. I didn't see where they went. Find them! Find them!"

Toby wriggled towards the hedge at his side, dragging his useless foot behind him. He pulled at the leaves, searching for a gap in the foliage, but it was dense and impenetrable. *Where the heck was Skylark? Why wasn't she returning for him? After all he had done for that arrogant, ungrateful witch!*

Something moved a few metres in front. A face appeared in the hedge. *Was that … Mrs Winterberry?* His next-door neighbour? A hand joined the head and beckoned wildly to him. Toby froze. Should he go? The torches bobbed closer, and the air around him thickened with smoke. He had no choice. Feeling he might be about to make things even worse, Toby slithered towards the head.

All at once, the heavens opened, and a torrent of rain fell from the sky. Within moments, Toby was drenched and could barely see through the sheets of water. As he continued his slow progress towards the face, he was soon swimming in mud. The head withdrew, leaving a hole at the bottom of the hedge. Toby had half pushed himself into the gap when a firm hand grasped his shoulder and pulled him through.

On the other side, Toby staggered to his feet, leaning against the hedge to minimise the sharp pain shooting through his leg. He was in Mrs Winterberry's garden. And it was indeed his next-door neighbour who had rescued him and who now stood beside him. Did she want to help him? Or did she have something else in mind?

She gestured towards her house. With Toby using her arm for support, the two of them shuffled up the garden. As they reached the back door, the rain stopped as abruptly as it had started. The red and orange glow had faded, leaving the blue blaze of the emergency vehicles lighting up the sky. The fire was out.

In Mrs Winterberry's kitchen, she helped Toby to a chair before tugging the curtains closed and turning on the light. "We don't want to attract any attention now, do we?" she muttered. Then she snatched the sodden balaclava from his head. "As I thought," she said, when his face popped into view.

The two of them eyed each other whilst copious amounts of muddy water trickled and dripped from their clothes, forming dirty puddles on the tiled floor. Toby waited for Mrs Winterberry to speak: to tell him off, to explain why she'd saved him. But she kept silent, looking just as uneasy as Toby.

With a small bang, a door appeared in the kitchen wall, and Willow, Bumble, Hazel, Skylark and Daisy rushed through from Toby's adjoining house. They too had been caught by the rainstorm and were drenched.

"Toby ..." began Witch Willow before her attention was distracted by the sight of Mrs Winterberry. "Witch Holly!"

"Witch Willow!" cried Mrs Winterberry.

Toby looked in confusion at the two women as they stared at each other in a mixture of surprise and delight.

Willow was the first to recover her power of speech. "What are you doing here?! What happened to you?" she asked Toby's neighbour.

"It was the SMI. They caught us. I managed to escape, but Ivy and Daisy were left behind. I've been watching and waiting for them for two years now."

Just then, she saw Daisy enveloped in the folds of Skylark's cloak. "Daisy! You're alive!" She held out her arms, but Daisy, overwhelmed by everything that had happened, clung to her sister.

"Why didn't you come back to Little Witchery?" Willow asked Mrs Winterberry.

"I couldn't. I didn't have my broom or my wand to get there. Or my warbler to navigate. So I stayed here, hoping I would see some sign of my sister and hoping I would be able to warn any other witch who might stray too close. Is Ivy not with you too?"

"No ..." replied Willow, her voice catching.

"She wasn't in the building then?" Mrs Winterberry turned to Toby.

He was at a loss for words. What could he say?

What had Willow said when she showed him Witch Ivy's house? '*It is clear to see ... that Witch Ivy is no longer alive.*' Images swam into Toby's mind: the operating theatre, the jars in the fridges. He could never mention them to Mrs Winterberry.

He was saved from having to reply by Willow. "We have a lot to catch up on," she assured Mrs Winterberry. "However, now is not the time. We must get away from here immediately."

"Toby," the Head Witch gave him a warm smile, "I cannot begin to tell you how grateful we are for your help and I must apologise for the behaviour of Witch Skylark. The destruction of Earthen buildings is by no means permitted under wyline law." Willow glared at the sullen looking witch by her side. "I did my best with the rain. I fear it came too late to save the building, but the fire at least is extinguished. Now, give me your shoes and balaclava and anything else that might identify you as having been at the SMI. We'll take them with us until the commotion has died down. Witch Holly you will, of course, return with us to Little Witchery."

Toby handed over his hat, gloves and shoes. Reluctantly, he returned the magical tools which had helped him, the wand-thief and the secret-seeker that was now drained.

Skylark watched him without the slightest thank you or apology.

"I saved your life and you left me to get caught!"

Anger bubbled inside Toby.

Skylark glowered. But Daisy took in a deep breath before whispering, "Thank you, Toby. I knew not all Earthens were bad." She reached out a timid hand and, despite his recent soaking, he was filled with warmth.

Then Bumble squeezed his arm. "Thank you, Toby, for saving my nieces. I knew you could do it." She tore a blue patch from her dress and pushed it into his fingers. "To bandage your ankle." She pointed to the green tinge appearing on his leg.

Willow waved her wand over the group. A blast of hot air swirled around them, and droplets of water evaporated from their clothes and hair. Soon, Toby was dry although he could feel his hair sticking out at strange angles.

You didn't see Barnaby out there, did you?" asked Bumble, a frown creasing her forehead.

Toby gulped. "He saved us. He attacked the security guard and the dog ... well, dragon. We wouldn't have got away without him." He paused. "I'm sorry, Bumble, he didn't make it."

Bumble's eyes brimmed with tears and she let out a loud sob. "Barnaby! My beloved fluttermouse."

Daisy left her sister and folded herself into her aunt's arms.

Toby hobbled towards the new door in the kitchen wall.

'Stay safe, Toby,' whispered Witch Hazel.

"Keep a low profile," said Willow. "I promise we will return at some point but not for a while now."

Return? Toby's stomach contorted. He wasn't sure he ever wanted to see them again.

"You know the SMI Director has one of them too," remarked Skylark, staring at his back.

Toby stopped walking.

"One of those strange white tufts in his hair like you," the witch continued.

Toby spun round, surprise and curiosity getting the better of him. "It's not strange! It's just a bit of hair that has no colour." But it *was* unusual. He'd never come across anybody else with it ... until now. Of all the people to have something in common with, the Director of the SMI, hunter of witches, would not be top of his list.

"Well, never mind. As Toby says, some people have it," interjected Willow. "We must leave now, but I think we'll make a small stop at 84 Lewis Road on our way home."

What? Of course! Toby was supposed to be meeting Dacker and Boz. Well this proved it – Willow *had* followed him to the park last night. She must have eavesdropped on the whole conversation too!

"I don't think that's a good idea," Toby said. Right now, the video of his mum would be a molten mass, smoking in the embers of the fire. Dacker and Boz no longer had any power over him. They could wait all night at Mr McClean's house, Toby had no intention of turning up.

"Don't worry," said Willow. "It'll be nothing to do with you. But somebody needs to teach them a little lesson."

Toby tried to protest, but Willow ushered him through the door into his kitchen. As he stepped through, it disappeared behind him, leaving him alone in the darkness.

So that was that then.

Apart from the occasional shout from the SMI grounds, an oppressive silence reigned. It bore down on Toby. After all the hustle and bustle, after all he'd seen and experienced, he was suddenly alone with his thoughts and his fears. And such a silence could feed those thoughts and fears. Toby leant on the kitchen counter staring into the darkness. Skylark had destroyed the SMI. What would happen to him and Mum? At once, his mind started to do what it always did: close down, stop thinking and stop feeling.

But NO!

Toby could not return to dealing with things by ignoring them. In the end, that didn't solve anything, it just made it worse. If he hid his thoughts at the back of his mind, they would grow into giant snakes of worry writhing around inside. They would plague him like the memory of Witch Ivy at the SMI window had haunted him. He needed to face what had happened. But not tonight, it was past midnight. He should get to bed and at least try to pretend he had been there all the time.

Toby limped to the bottom of the stairs. With his ankle as it was, the staircase loomed in front of him, a steep mountain to climb. Step by step, he half-crawled, half-hauled himself upstairs, attempting to make no noise. He couldn't bear to see Mum right now. With any luck, she would be fast asleep. At the top, he let out a deep breath. A few more steps and then he would be in the safety of his bedroom. One step, two steps …

"Toby?" came his mum's weak call.

Clenching his teeth, he hobbled into her bedroom.

She was wide awake and pale. "I heard sirens! What happened? How did it go?"

Toby shuffled over to the window and drew aside the curtains before sinking onto the bed.

"You're hurt! Are you OK? Toby! Tell me what happened!"

He looked out of the window; the fire had died down, but smoke still billowed in the air and blue flashing lights illuminated the sky. "There's been a fire at the SMI."

"A fire? ... A big fire?" His mum's face went deathly white.

Toby felt sick with guilt. "It was Skylark. She wasn't supposed to destroy the building! I tried to stop her, honest I did, Mum. But she'd gone kind of wild and uncontrollable."

"Did you get her out?"

"Yes. They were going to start experimenting on

her tomorrow! And her little sister, Daisy, was there too."

They sat in silence while activity buzzed behind the back hedge and the acrid air burnt their throats … and their hearts.

"Are the witches safe now?" There was tenderness in his mum's voice.

"Yes," whispered Toby.

CHAPTER TWENTY-EIGHT

Dacker and Boz sat on the wall outside Mr. McClean's house.

"Bean's late!" growled Boz.

"Mmm," murmured Dacker.

A noise came from their right.

"What was that?" Boz whipped his head around, trying to see through the shadows.

A large pebble rolled towards them, coming to a stop by their feet.

They frowned at each other. Footsteps marched right up to them. Footsteps which didn't belong to anyone.

"Hallo-o-o-o," whispered a voice in Boz's ear.

The two boys shot upright as if their backsides were on fire. They began to run, but somehow their shoes had become tied together. Dacker stumbled forwards, and Boz crashed down on top of him.

"Gerroff!" shrieked Dacker, flattened on the floor.

Across the street, a lid fell from a dustbin and clattered to the ground. Lights flew on in the nearby houses. Yanking off their entangled shoes and pulling themselves to their feet, Dacker and Boz sprinted up the street, barefoot and racing for home.

They didn't hear the snorting chuckle that Bumble just couldn't contain.

CHAPTER TWENTY-NINE

The next morning, Toby answered the door to find a policeman standing outside. "We're doing house calls," he said in a gruff voice. "Investigating the arson attack at the SMI last night. I don't suppose you saw anything?"

Toby mumbled a non-committal reply.

"The security guard was able to give us a lot of information," continued the man. "Interestingly, the suspect is about your height. Where were you around midnight yesterday evening?"

"I was here," Toby replied. He tried to look the policeman straight in the eye, thankful his voice stayed steady and didn't let him down this time. There came a tinkle from above: Bat-ears upstairs was listening. "I need to see what my mum wants."

"It's essential we talk to everybody who lives here," declared the unwelcome visitor.

"She's not well enough." Leaving the policeman standing on the step, Toby limped up the stairs.

"How did you hurt yourself?" the man called after him.

"I fell down the stairs." Toby retreated before he could be questioned further.

A few seconds later, he returned. "My mum will see you for a moment."

The policeman entered the bedroom and stood awkwardly at the door.

With the help of Toby, his mum propped herself up in bed and cleared her throat. "Officer," she began in an authoritative yet dignified voice that Toby had not heard since she was well. "You're wasting your time here. My son had nothing to do with the destruction of the SMI. Around the time the building was going up in flames, he was helping me to the bathroom. So please put your efforts to better use and find the hooligans that did this!"

Under her withering look, the policeman wilted like a schoolboy being reprimanded by his teacher. "I … we … that is …" the man stuttered. "My number." He placed his card on the bed. "In case you need to contact us." He scuttled out of the room and down the stairs.

Toby stared at his mum in astonishment and admiration. When the front door had banged shut, she slumped back on her pillows. "Well," she said, "it was only half a lie." She suppressed a small, wicked smile. "After all, you weren't responsible for the SMI destruction."

Toby sat down on the bed next to her. "Will we lose our income?"

"I don't know, but we'll survive. I'm proud of you, Toby. You did the right thing." She patted his hand.

For once, he didn't pull away. He kept hold of her hand, and his insides thawed a little, enough to ask the question that had been eating away at him. "If the authorities find out you're ill, find out I have to do everything ..." Toby hesitated, "will they take me away?" He chewed the inside of his lip and stared at the duvet.

"Of course not! Wherever did you get that idea? If anything, they'll give us help, so you don't have to do so much."

"I don't want to tell them! Don't tell them! I can manage."

"OK, sweetheart, let's see how it goes, hey?" She pulled him towards her and hugged him.

"I wish you weren't ill. I wish Dad was here," Toby whispered.

"I know, my love." She stroked his hair. "But don't worry, we'll be alright. Whatever happens, we'll cope. We have each other, right? And that's all that matters."

Toby let his body relax. For the first time in ages, Mum was in charge. Soon he'd have to get back to the household chores but not just yet. He rested his head on her shoulder and closed his eyes.

CHAPTER THIRTY

"Sisters, we are persecuted. We removed ourselves from Earth, but still we are attacked, we are killed. It is clear now that Earthens are aware of our existence and they will not tolerate it. We are safe no longer." Ebonia's voice boomed throughout the main hall. "We are lucky that Witches Holly, Skylark and Daisy are with us now, back in our home. However, Witch Ivy is lost forever. Who will be next?" She paused, giving time for her words to sink in to the listening clan. "We cannot hide away any longer. Join with me. It's time to unite. It's time to show what our magic can do. It's time for action."

Witches all over the auditorium cheered. They held up their wands, and an explosion of bangs filled the air. Ebonia sat down, a smug smile concealed on her lips.

"Sizzling serpents," muttered Bumble. "This is not good, not good at all."

Daisy sat next to her, holding tightly to her mum on the other side. She hadn't let go since they'd returned to Little Witchery.

Willow stood up, looking as calm and poised as ever. "Thank you, Ebonia," she said, "for that invigorating speech." She faced the audience. "There is no denying that some Earthens pose a risk. But how big is this risk, I ask you? The SMI, the organisation that captured Witches Skylark, Daisy and Holly, has been destroyed. And let us not forget, it was an Earthen himself who was the one to rescue them. To him, we will always be grateful. Fighting is not the way forward. War is not the way forward. The loss of life on our side would be immense. Yes, we have a power that Earthens do not possess. But they outnumber us by millions to one. They have weapons that would destroy Little Witchery in an instant. New killer bombs, I believe they are called." Willow's eyes scanned the crowd, making contact with every single witch. "Sisters, I have served and protected you for ten years. Let me continue to do so. Our future safety is my number one priority."

A hush fell over the clan. Bumble searched their faces. Witches muttered between themselves, but no one called out. It was up to her. She stood so quickly, her chair clattered over.

"Willow for Head Witch!" she cried at the top of her voice. She pointed her wand at the ceiling. A jet of red shot into the air and burst into a cloud of red smoke.

Other witches jumped to their feet. "Willow for Head Witch! Willow for Head Witch!" they chorused. Red sparks and mist flooded the auditorium.

219

Then a witch at the back shouted, "Ebonia for Head Witch!" and a stream of green shot from her wand. Others joined her. The hall swirled with red and green as if an explosion of fireworks had been set off.

Soon, every witch over the age of sixteen had voted and every pair of eyes stared at the sky. The smoke dispersed. Who would it be? Red for Willow? Or green for Ebonia? It was so silent, Bumble could hear her own breathing. It was going to be red, no green, no …

The air cleared until only a pale red vapour lingered. The green had gone. The crowd erupted. Willow had won, just. Bumble collapsed onto her chair, wiping beads of sweat from her brow. *Bubbling cauldrons, that had been close.*

Later, Willow sat at her desk and pulled out a piece of paper. With a flourish, she began to write: *Dear Toby …*

CHAPTER THIRTY-ONE

That evening, Toby opened the door to find Roger and Jazz outside. He shot them a quizzical look. His friends hardly ever came over these days.

"Well, we've no idea what you did to Dacker and Boz last night," said Jazz, "but they were terrified!"

"They were?"

"Didn't you see their reaction?" She held out her phone. "I got it on camera!"

Toby watched the screen as Dacker fell over. The look on his face when Boz flattened him to the floor! Toby saw the dustbin lid clatter to the ground, the two boys scramble to their feet and race petrified up the street. Toby giggled. He hit rewind. And watched again. And again. *Five to Toby.*

Roger and Jazz beamed to see their friend happy.

"Make sure you keep the video," said Toby. "Just in case we ever need to threaten them with it." It would be good to give Dacker and Boz a taste of their own medicine for a change.

"Guess what!" cried Roger. He couldn't contain his excitement any longer. "I got into Radton

Rangers!"

Toby's insides plummeted. He knew he should be pleased for Roger, but Radton Rangers was Toby's football club! He'd been their best player and now Roger, who was so much slower with the ball, was going to play for them.

Roger shoved a plastic bag into Toby's hands. "Cheer up, Tobe," he said. "You're going to play for them too!"

"What …?" stammered Toby.

"They know you haven't played properly for a while, but they want you back. They've been missing their star striker."

"I can't!" shouted Toby. "You know I can't. I can't get there and I can't leave Mum in the evenings. She's already at home all day by herself and I have to make her dinner."

"My mum's going to drive us." Roger was triumphant. "And then she's going to get your mum dinner. Two evenings a week and Saturday afternoons. It's all arranged. And the season doesn't start for another month, so plenty of time for your foot to heal." He indicated Toby's bandaged ankle. "Just don't go falling down any more stairs, alright?"

As they turned to leave, Jazz said, "We're cycling to the river tomorrow. Want to come?"

Toby opened his mouth to say no. Then paused. Mum wouldn't need him all day. In fact, she'd be glad of some quiet. What was stopping him?

"We'll make sure we go at a time that's right for your mum; so you can still do her meals. We could help you cook, if you wanted," said Jazz.

An overwhelming mix of emotions bubbled up in Toby. "OK. That would be good," he replied in a strangled voice. "Thanks, guys."

Toby took the plastic bag up to his room before he dared open it. He pulled out a brand new Radton Rangers kit. It was dark blue and white stripes. It hadn't changed a bit in the two years he'd been absent. On the back, the word 'Bean' was inscribed over the number nine. His old number! Toby held the top to his cheek as the silent tears fell.

He peered into his mum's bedroom to find her peeping over the covers with a broad grin on her face.

"You knew about this?" he asked.

She nodded. Before she could say anything, something banged on the window, and they both jumped. A large yellow creature hovered outside, its wings flapping. *Was that Cuddles?* Toby opened the window and the bird-dog flew in. It landed on the bed, making his mum bounce up and down.

"What the ...?" she exclaimed.

Cuddles' head nestled Toby's hand.

"What are you doing here? Does Bumble know?" Toby stroked him, and his fingers hit a scroll of paper attached to the collar. He opened it to reveal elegant lines of writing, slanting across the page.

Dear Toby,

We are immensely grateful for your help in rescuing Witches Skylark and Daisy. And we are sorry for any trouble it may have caused you. We are keen to return the favour. Witch Hazel and Witch Bumble request your permission to visit twice a week to help with household chores etc.

Please send your reply by Golden Retrieagle.

Silver wishes,
Witch Willow, Head Witch

"What is it?" asked Mum.

"It's the witches … they want to help out." Toby showed her the note.

"That's kind! And a big risk for them to come down again. They must be very grateful to you. Maybe we should accept, if you're sure you can trust them."

"Mmm …"

"I *am* worrying a bit about Roger's mum making my meals while you're at football. She has enough to do with her own brood."

Part of Toby recoiled at the thought of seeing the witches again. They'd brought him so much trouble. Yet, a spark of excitement fizzed in his chest. Now that he knew magic existed, knew that a town of witches lived in the sky, the idea of carrying on with his mundane life as if nothing had happened seemed inconceivable.

Another bang on the window pane, a smaller one this time, as if a bird had flown into the glass. Toby opened it and in fluttered a very dazed, very bedraggled bat.

"Barnaby!" cried Toby. "You're alive!"

The bat slumped on the duvet and let out a low groan. Toby dipped his finger in the glass of water by his mum's bed and held it over Barnaby's mouth. The exhausted creature stuck out his tongue and gulped.

Well that settled it. Toby would have to see the witches again, even if only to return Bumble's bat. She was going to be over the moon.

He looked at his mum. "And you're sure you're OK with it? With having the witches here? I know other people wear you out." An image of Witch Hazel standing in their sprugel splattered kitchen flew into Toby's mind and he banished it hastily. Best not to mention that to Mum … or let the witches use the oven again.

"This illness might have stopped my life, sweetheart. But I don't want it to suffocate yours too. So, if it means you get to play football, then I'm more than OK with it. In fact, I insist." And, for the first time in a long time, his mum's eyes were smiling too.

KEEP AN EYE OUT FOR THE NEXT BOOK IN THE SERIES:

TOBY AND THE WIZARD SLAVES

COMING 2022

M.E.

An estimated 250,000 people in the UK live with M.E. and an estimated 17 million worldwide.

They suffer from a wide range of symptoms including physical fatigue, brain fatigue, muscle aches, flu-like symptoms, headaches, lightheadedness, sleep problems and more.

Approximately one quarter of these people have Severe or Very Severe M.E., like Toby's mum. They are housebound and often bedbound.

There has been very little research into M.E. and there is no treatment and no cure. Yet M.E. is a very real illness which has destroyed the lives of countless individuals and their families.

A minority of people recover from M.E., but the majority suffer for years and decades, left alone to try and deal with their illness as best they can.

If you or a loved one are suffering with M.E., please remember you are not alone. For information and support, check out the two main charities in the UK:

www.actionforme.org.uk
www.meassociation.org.uk

Ten percent of the profits of this book will be donated to the M.E. Association to raise much needed funds for research and support.

YOUNG CARERS

There are an estimated 800,000 young carers in the UK. Young carers, like Toby, are responsible for looking after a family member who is ill, or looking after other family members, such as siblings, to support the ill person.

Young carers often have to do household chores and have less free time to spend with their friends and on hobbies. They might have to miss school and are more likely to be bullied.

If you are a young carer, you might feel like you're alone, but you are not. You can talk to your teacher, a school nurse or your GP. You can also find advice and support at:

www.childrenssociety.org.uk/information/young-people/young-carers

ABOUT THE AUTHOR

(Photo credit to Katie Lister Photography)

Sally Doherty lives in leafy Surrey with her husband and three-legged (but speedy) rescue dog. After studying French and German at university, she worked for a year in London before unexpectedly falling ill with M.E. Being stuck at home and often in bed for fifteen years, however, has lit a cauldron of stories bubbling inside her imagination.

TOBY AND THE SILVER BLOOD WITCHES is her debut book and the first in a trilogy.

FOLLOW SALLY ONLINE

Twitter
@Sally_writes

Facebook
www.facebook.com/sallydohertywrites

Website
www.sallydohertyauthor.com

Sign up to the newsletter to be the first to hear about giveaways and book two!

If you or a family member has M.E. and want to connect, you can also find Sally tweeting about life with chronic illness @SallyClareR.

ACKNOWLEDGEMENTS

I have so many people to thank for helping my book (and me) get this far:

First and foremost, my mum. For believing in Toby from the very beginning, many years ago now. And for the countless hours she has spent editing and providing a second opinion. And basically being my all-round support. Thank you, thank you, thank you. We did it!

My sister. For being one of the first people to read Toby in its early stages and for being my rock in this unwelcome journey of M.E. we share. You are an inspirational strength. Love you, sis. And my eight year old nephew, Thomas, for being the most excited person when he heard my book was being published, and for being such a wonderful addition to our family.

My husband. For being my sounding board night after night, despite a busy day at work. And for his years of love, support, humour, cooking and dog-walking as we navigate this illness and life together. (Are you going to read the book now?)

My dad. For his love and support throughout the years (and his questionable jokes).

My illustrator, Sarah Jane Docker. Who has designed the most beautiful cover, map and characters and brought my book to life. Thank you so much.

My writing friends, in particular Anna Britton and my writing group (in no particular order!): Marisa Noelle,

Emma Read, Lorna Riley, Stuart White, Caroline Murphy, Ellie Lock, Lydia Massiah and Anna Orridge. For your critiques, support, banter, and humour on this rollercoaster writing journey and in life in general. I (and Toby) would be lost without you.

And to the many lovely people on Twitter who I interact with on a daily basis – Emma Bradley and too many others to name but you know who you are!

Ayesha at Whittle Critique, and Emma Finlayson-Palmer and Jeanna Skinner at Wonder Writers. For your full manuscript critiques which were instrumental in improving my book.

Caleb and Silas Brown and Jess Porter – my first child readers. For your feedback and enthusiasm and giving me the confidence to hit publish.

My childhood and university friends and family-in-law. For being so supportive and enthusiastic as soon as I dared tell anyone I was writing a book. Hayley Andrews, Becky Chumun, Katie Lister, Fiona Biermann, Emily Kirkpatrick, Clare Brown, Lucy Sheehan, Maggie Rudduck, Shaun Rudduck.

Oh, and of course, to you my reader, if you've made it this far. For buying and reading Toby. I hope you enjoyed it.

Printed in Great Britain
by Amazon